THE STOLEN IMAGE

Alexei Baran is the notoriously difficult, publicity-shy star of the Imperial Ballet. On the strength of her previous pictures of him, Anna, a photographer, is asked to portray the ballet company at work. Almost in self-defence she becomes engaged to James Farmer, but this proves to be no protection at all against falling in love with Baran. But when he discovers how she has used his captured image, Alexei is determined that she should steal no more of him . . .

ELAINE DANIEL

---◆---

THE STOLEN IMAGE

Complete and Unabridged

LINFORD
Leicester

First published in Great Britain in 1974 by
Robert Hale Limited
London

First Linford Edition
published 2008
by arrangement with
Robert Hale Limited
London

British Library CIP Data

Daniel, Elaine
  The stolen image.—Large print ed.—
Linford romance library
  1. Woman photographers—Fiction
  2. Ballet dancers—Fiction 3. Love stories
  4. Large type books
  I. Title
  823.9'14 [F]

  ISBN 978–1–84782–337–3

Published by
F. A. Thorpe (Publishing)
Anstey, Leicestershire

Set by Words & Graphics Ltd.
Anstey, Leicestershire
Printed and bound in Great Britain by
T. J. International Ltd., Padstow, Cornwall

This book is printed on acid-free paper

1

For the first time since she had come to London, Anna had to admit to feeling lonely.

It was a gentle, elegiac autumn day, the air still tenderly veiled with a morning mist through which the reddish golden sun shone as if through gauze. Far below Anna's flat among the rooftops, the great city stirred and restlessly moved, but with a muted sound as if everyone, everywhere, had fallen under the spell of the same soft melancholy.

Such a reaction was bound to come, she consoled herself, padding barefoot from her bed through to the tiny, box-like kitchen and switching on the kettle. She couldn't expect to go on as though the rest of her life were to be one glorious holiday. A month was long enough to have spent in London entirely alone without any plans or any direction. It had seemed at first impossible that she should ever tire of it, of the crowds, the moods of the city, its buildings and shops and parks, the sense one had of many villages all grown together, still different and yet all somehow recognisable as London. She had thought that she would never weary of evenings spent at the theatre, at concerts. It ought to be enough for anyone loving ballet as she did, to live so close to the Imperial Theatre that the great bulk of its enormous stage tower almost blocked her view of the sky. But now, quite suddenly, it wasn't enough. True, she could go every night if she wished and sit and watch some of the greatest dancers in the world as they moved superbly through the rituals of their art; she could wait afterwards in the dark outside the stage door, squashed and jostled among dozens of others as ardent and as star-struck as she, until the gods appeared and briefly walked among them. But that wasn't what she wanted. That left her still on the outside looking in, and that was where she had been all her life, and she was tired of it.

When the father she had never known had died and left her a considerable sum of money — more than she could ever have hoped to acquire by any normal means — her immediate and only thought had been to leave Midhampton and come to London. There were no ties to keep her. Since her mother's death no one had needed her and she had no real home — a room in a pleasant enough house with a warm-hearted landlady and a friendly visiting cat, but nothing of her own. Her job with a local photographer had been agreeable but dull, affording her in the weekly round of weddings, family groups and baby portraits little opportunity to use her creative flair or to develop any really personal style in photography. All the same, she had been reasonably happy and it had taught her a great deal. Dreams, after all, have a way of sounding foolish when put into words, and she had learned by now not to try to explain, even when asked, the ambition that gnawed at her and made her restless; it was as well not to say to the solid citizens of Midhampton that one's imagination took fire from the world of the dance, and that to photograph ballet — to catch and freeze and make permanent the fleeting, perfect movement, to pluck beauty from the air — was the most desirable thing in the whole of life. Even to herself, when she tried to see it with their eyes, it seemed a strange desire.

It might all have been different if she had ever been taught to dance. But Midhampton was not a town where so exotic an art as ballet naturally flourished, and there was no theatre. Even if there had been, and if Anna could have seen ballet on stage so as to recognise what she wanted, she would certainly have been rejected for any serious training as being too tall, a large and ungainly child clearly not built for dancing. Besides, they had been poor; her mother, deserted when Anna was yet small, had sometimes found the struggle merely to survive a hard enough fight. There had been nothing for extras. Yet all that time, as far away from them as he could get, in America, Anna's father had been making a modest but solid fortune.

Even now that a great deal of the fortune had come to her, Anna could not help feeling bitter. She could not think of her father without resentment, nor of her mother without pain. Observation of her mother's suffering had built into her a deep suspicion of all that concerned love and marriage; it seemed to her a gamble, with the odds very heavily weighted against women. Also, from being a lumpy, rather plain child she had grown into a tall girl, not immediately or obviously pretty and without the self-confidence necessary to carry off her very real but unusual dark beauty. Men tended not to notice her, or, if despite all her attempts to fade into the background they did so, were uncertain of how they should approach her. Anna avoided them. Much safer, more romantic was that magical, reflected world, more dream than waking, where every emotion was noble and even sadness became transfigured by music and by the dancers' art into something profoundly beautiful.

Sometimes she suspected that for her the theatre was a means of escape, a release for dreams she dared not pin on anything more real. But knowing that it worked that way did nothing to lessen the attraction for her of the glittering greasepaint magnet. Freed from anything that tied her to Midhampton, she had made for the densest thicket of theatres that she knew, and had landed in Bloom Street, between Covent Garden and Kingsway, near to the Opera House and to Drury Lane and even closer to the Imperial, whose blank and forbidding back wall towered over the narrow road and overshadowed all but the topmost windows of the tall houses. Up among the rooftops Anna had sunshine for most of the day, but even on her at sunset the shadow of the great theatre fell.

Her flat was a ramshackle collection of box-like attics, chiefly appealing to her because of the proximity of the theatre which housed one of the world's principal ballet companies, but also because it had a spare room in which there was a wash-basin, perfect for a dark-room. By one of those odd coincidences with which life abounds, the flat's previous tenant, a journalist and writer, had started his career on the staff of the *Midshire Gazette*, the same weekly paper in which many of Anna's wedding photographs smudgily saw the light. He had been full of enthusiastic memories of the 'good old *Gazette*' and had promised to look Anna up once she had settled in, but she discounted the promise since he was a very trendy young man clearly well on his way up in the world and she could not imagine why he should want to waste his time on her. There was no one else she could claim to know in the whole of London.

Alone, she had equipped the dark-room first, becoming slightly giddy in the realisation that she could afford almost any equipment she wanted — within reason, and always allowing for the fact that the room was scarcely more than a cupboard. It seemed reasonable to buy well; she had no absolute need to work for some time yet, but in that time she hoped possibly to make a name for herself, in a modest way, so that a career would have been well founded by the time that it mattered to her to have one. Looking ahead, therefore, she bought the best enlargers she could, and carefully selected all the rest to match their standard, and then paid the enormous bill without much more than a passing qualm. The window of the little room was now permanently shuttered with hardboard and painted a dull navy blue to match the walls and the ceiling. Shiny red box shelves lined one wall, and the working bench had red-fronted cupboards beneath it where chemicals could be stored. The washbasin was replaced by a large, square sink. It was, perhaps, the most elegant dark-room in the whole Covent Garden area; it was certainly the most elegant room in the flat, since Anna's energies had been so much devoted to making it perfect that she had not yet thought what to do with the rest. The walls everywhere else were still a sad porridge colour marked by dingy patchwork squares where the previous tenant's pictures had hung. The windows had as yet no curtains, nor the floors any better covering than ancient brown lino and a few thin rugs. The bedroom had a bed with a knobbly brass bedstead, a white wardrobe, a stripped pine chest of drawers and a large poster of Margot Fonteyn in *Giselle*. Opening from it and sharing with it the awesome view of the Imperial's mountainous bulk, the sitting-room contained a large black sofa and two strange sack-like objects full of granules which theoretically one punched into a comfortable shape to sit on; she had bought them on impulse and was inclined now to regret it, having failed so far to come to any acceptable agreement with them as to what constituted comfort. There were some deep box shelves and a great many books. A lonely television set stood in one corner. It wasn't very homely, but somehow there seemed to have been no time apart from equipping the dark-room and then sight-seeing and theatre-going; she spent little time in the flat except for eating and sleeping, and occasionally developing and printing the photographs she had taken on her various excursions, pinning these up on walls about the flat until she tired of seeing them and replaced them with others.

The kitchen, where she waited now for the kettle to boil and then made a pot of strong coffee, was pleasant; it looked down on the tiny gardens between the backs of Bloom Street houses and those in the next row. No one bothered to tend these little patches of ground, and yet trees still grew, lilac, laburnum and roses among all the litter of dustbins and discarded cartons, old broken furniture and the occasional line of faintly depressed-looking washing. The back windows of the other houses were by day blank and uninformative, as she supposed her own must be. But by night one caught glimpses here and there of other people's lives in lighted rooms before the curtains were drawn. Many of the windows always remained dark; offices or shops occupied most of the lower floors in this area. It was a vigorous, cosmopolitan neighbourhood teeming with theatrical costumiers, Greek and Italian restaurants, bookshops, office stationers, coffee and food shops, jewellers — almost every strange and exotic thing one could think of, and, Anna suspected, a number that out of sheer inexperience she could not even begin to imagine. Soho, after all, was not far away. Her own house had an importer's offices on the first two floors and flats above that. She had never met her downstairs neighbours; they came and went mysteriously, and all she knew about them was that they were called Rodzinska and got through three pints of milk a day.

It was a good place to be, she thought now, pouring out her first cup of coffee. She loved the area and the flat; this little kitchen felt like home to her by now, cheerfully brown and orange and white, and somehow more lived-in than any of the other rooms. The cooker was fairly new and bore scarcely a trace of use. The bottle rack in the fridge, on the other hand, was much scratched and battered, and she had come upon a whole crate of empties in the bottom of a cupboard. Judging by that, and by the many cigarette burns on the lino and the circular marks on the shelves above the radiators, she concluded that James Farmer, late of the *Midshire Gazette*, had lived a satisfactorily merry social life.

As her habit was, she wandered with her mug of coffee out of the kitchen, across the hall and into the sitting-room. Her bare feet made a faint padding sound on the chilly lino. She pulled her long red corduroy dressing-gown closer round her and wondered if summer were really over, and what winter in London would be like. The mist beyond her window was already clearing. She looked out at the huge brick container that was the Imperial, and wished, as she wished every day, that she could see the stage door from here. Then she might watch the stars arriving, every morning see Blaise and Baran, Krainov, Raimann, dancers of such magnitude coming to the theatre for classes and rehearsals. But the stage door was out of sight; all that she could see was a blank brick wall and a jutting staircase block built out from the main building, obscuring her view of the side of the theatre where the stage entrance was.

The staircase terminated in a little railed-in area of flat roof, a balcony sheltering under the rising bulk of the stage tower, and sometimes men in shirt sleeves came out through a skylight door and puffed at a quick cigarette, looking down without much interest at the cars and people in the street below. One day one of them had looked across at Anna's window and caught her looking out as she was doing now; she had blushed guiltily, quickly hiding the camera with which she had been stalking him, seeing a good subject for a picture. Impossible to explain her built-in instinct to reach for a camera; at least, impossible to explain it to a stage-hand on a roof the width of a street away. He had smiled at her and waved, and had gone then, leaving her longing to be able to follow him down into the theatre, into the exciting noise and smell of back-stage, to watch the ballet company at work.

This morning the light was clear yet mellow, making the shadows among the rooftops cool wells of shade; a perfect day for taking her camera out and wandering about London, plenty of even light, plenty of contrast —

There was someone already on the little roof balcony of the theatre. Not a stage-hand, surely; a figure so still that one might easily fail to see it, curiously swathed from head to foot in a greyish cloak which was drawn round and over one shoulder and held there by a pale, motionless hand. Apart from this, only the head was visible, the face turned down and away from the light. Very gently the breeze caught and ruffled the edges of a mane of dark hair and nudged a fold of the heavy cloak. Otherwise it might have been a marble statue, or perhaps some misplaced theatrical prop or a shop window dummy.

Straining her eyes to discern features in the averted face, Anna felt a growing excitement which tingled through her and made the cold morning suddenly warm. Before the head began slowly to turn, before its features were revealed to the clear, steady light, she knew whose face she would see. Leaning against the high wall of the stage tower and looking now up at the sky, every muffled line of his body eloquent with despair, stood Alexei Baran.

He was a dancer spoken of in the same breath as Nijinsky and Nureyev. He was the personification of fame, glamour and mystery, a man who revealed nothing of himself, claiming to be nothing outside of his work, and who therefore attracted to every small detail of his life the remorseless searchlight of public curiosity. He was more photographed than perhaps any other dancer, and hated photographs. He was widely quoted but refused to be interviewed. At twenty-eight he was handsome, virile, and tantalisingly unmarried — a gift, in short, to the myth-makers. Anna's reaction to seeing him, once astonishment had passed, was the instinctive response of a photographer; she grabbed for her camera. By chance it was already fitted with the long-distance lens, a kind of telescope which brought distant objects into close-up. She found herself focusing upon Alexei Baran's magnificently photogenic face as though she herself stood no more than a few feet away from him. It was a highcheekboned Slav face, with straight, wide-winged brows and eyes below them of a disconcertingly dark and mysterious grey, fringed with thick black lashes. The nose was straight, imperious, the mouth generous and finely moulded, the chin perfectly proportioned and firm. It was a face of contradictions, at one moment proud, at the next tender; it could light up with joy or darken in an anger that struck like a thunderbolt. It was, in fact, the perfect dancer's face, able to express anything it might be called on to express and yet remain always magnificent to look at. Anna, who loved faces, found that she could not contemplate this one without a kind of constriction about the heart, to think that any human could be so splendidly made.

At this moment, alone high above the seething world of busy streets and theatres, Baran stood believing himself to be unobserved, and the superb and world-famous features were stripped of all pretence. What they revealed to the unseeing sky and to illicitly watching Anna, was a deep bone-weariness, a look as though life were a long ache to be endured, and endurance almost ended. It was an utterly private moment, a revelation of unhappiness that the world was not meant to see; and Anna photographed it. Her battle with her conscience was brief. She could no more have resisted the urge to get that face on film than she could have resisted the urge to breathe.

She took several shots of his profile etched medallion-like against the dark theatre roof, his eyes brooding on the impersonal panorama of rooftops and chimneys, tendrils of longish hair flickering in the breeze like black flames about his head. She changed lenses and took full-length shots. And then, disconcertingly, he turned and looked straight into the eye of the camera.

She dropped out of sight below the windowsill so quickly that he must have had scarcely time enough to register what he had seen. Like a criminal on the run she crouched there, her heart banging like a steam hammer. When she finally summoned the courage to raise her head and peep over the window-ledge, the balcony opposite was empty, the door to the theatre firmly closed.

Anna found that she was trembling, she did not know whether from excitement or from fear. It had all happened so suddenly; there had been no time to argue the rights and wrongs of deliberately spying on the private life of a public figure. But that was what it amounted to. It wasn't a nice thing to have to admit to herself, and reaction set in now, a feeling of guilt and uncertainty. Yet who in the world, caring as she did about pictures, could have resisted such a chance?

Panic swept her, in case she should prove to have misjudged the light or focused badly or shaken the camera. Hurriedly she changed from her night-wear into comfortable old jeans and a navy sweater, and gulped down the rest of the mug of by now cool coffee; then, carrying the camera rather as though it were an unexploded mine, she hurried into the darkroom and shut herself in. She removed the film from the camera and fed it into the developing tank; Baran's image must be processed like that of any other mortal. What seemed a long, long age later, after the film had gone through all the maddeningly slow stages of development, fixing, drying and at last printing, she looked at the pictures swimming in the hypo bath, and knew them for the shots of her lifetime. They revealed more about Alexei Baran than words could ever do. She held them up one by one and scanned them, scrutinising every inch of shiny, wet surface; her pulses ached with beating and a kind of awe crept over her at the thought that she had made these pictures. The problem, of course, having taken them, was what she should now do with them.

As she pondered this faintly dampening realisation, the doorbell of her flat distantly shrilled.

It was a sufficiently unusual occurrence for her to be startled out of all thought of Alexei Baran, photographs or instant journalistic fame. For a moment she stood rooted, mentally going through a short list of likely callers. The mikman didn't come for two days yet, and it wasn't the postman's normal time — and that about exhausted the possibilities. Someone collecting, perhaps — a flag seller, raffle tickets —

When she eventually got to the door and put an end to speculation by actually opening it, her caller proved to be James Farmer, late of the *Midshire Gazette* and the previous occupant of the flat. She felt quite weak with relief.

21

For one dizzy, terrifying moment as she unlatched the door she had been filled with a quite blindly unreasonable conviction that she would discover Alexei Baran standing there on her doorstep.

'I couldn't think who it could be!' she blurted out at him. 'There's no one normally comes at this time of day. I was in the dark-room. Really, it's good of you to come — I hadn't really expected — '

In her general astonishment and relief and confusion she was incoherent, quite disproportionately grateful to him, exclaiming again and again with surprise until he plaintively said:

'Really, it's nice to be so welcome, but would you rather I went away again till a more suitable moment? I mean, if there's a body in a cupboard you'd rather dispose of quietly, or a man under the bed — '

'Oh, don't go! I am demented, I know. It's wild excitement — I just took a good photograph — photographs — '

'Ah.' At once he understood. He would, she thought, having worked on a paper — even so dull a paper as the *Gazette*. 'Something newsworthy? A scoop?'

'Well — would you like to see?'

'Delighted.' He had been carrying a coat, and laid it aside now on the single chair that the hall contained. In some faintly surprised, still functioning part of her normal self Anna registered the fact that he was a very personable creature, if just a little too smoothly presented; immaculate grey flannel suit cut by an artist, toffee-coloured tie matching his toffee-coloured hair, palest blue shirt very nearly the same blue as his eyes, and charmingly regular features. Yet she felt scarcely able to see him for the picture of Alexei Baran that still burned on her retina.

She led the way into the dark-room, switching on the overhead light so that the results of her work could clearly be seen. James Farmer looked once approvingly round him and then turned his attention to the half-dozen or so prints in the dish.

'Wow!' Impressed, he leaned over them, gingerly lifting them by the tongs so that he could look more closely. He seemed to know what to look for; his pleasant but faintly vacuous face had sharpened into concentration and judgement. He looked entirely like a journalist.

'These are winners, aren't they?' he said eventually, when he had looked at the rest of the prints already washing. 'How did you come by them?'

She explained to him about the balcony. 'I keep worrying that I ought not to have done it.'

'Invading his privacy, you mean? Yes — but you could get away with it, you know, in almost any paper — '

'No.' She felt an actual sinking sensation, not so much where her heart was as in her stomach. Quite suddenly she knew that she could never use the photographs. 'He looks so terribly undefended. They're too revealing — I couldn't square it with myself, to send

them to a paper and have that —
whatever it is he's feeling — printed for
millions to gawp at over their corn-
flakes.'

'Dear, dear!' Mildly, James Farmer
shook his head at her. 'You'll never make
a news-hound.' He seemed, though, not
much distressed by the thought. He was
looking at the photographs again, and
had grown thoughtful. 'How do they
compare with your normal work?' he
wanted to know.

'I don't all that often find such
a subject. But they're technically on a
par. I do have a certain flair, I know
that — one has to know it.'

'Done any ballet or theatre work?'

'In Midhampton?'

He nodded, understanding. 'All the
same, if you had the chance — '

'Oh, it would be wonderful! Ballet is
a thing with me — an obsession, I
suppose.'

'What's anyone without an obsession
of some kind? One might as well not
live at all as not care fanatically about at

least one thing.' He turned back to the photographs. 'I've an idea.'

Anna suddenly comprehended the fact that his questions had been leading up to something. She felt all at once slightly sick, as though events had whirled her around too fast.

'I'm considering a project,' James Farmer began, 'for which I need a photographer. It's a series of books on the performing arts in London, now — a record of what's happening, what's to be seen by the cultured Londoner of the seventies. I shall do the text, but there must be pictures — lots and lots of pictures. I think you might be just the person I'm looking for.'

Anna opened her mouth, and no words came out of it. She stared at him in disbelief. It was so totally unexpected, and so near to the stuff of her wildest dreams, that she hardly dared to believe what she had heard.

'Think about it?' he urged. 'Or maybe you've something else lined up?'

'No! Oh, no — nothing. It's just so

— unexpected. But I don't need to think about whether I want to do it; only about whether or not I can. I mean, it's so far outside of anything I've ever done.'

'You could begin on the Imperial Ballet. I know Lensky, who runs the company. He doesn't mind cameras so long as they produce flattering results — he might even agree to our using these shots of Baran, one at least.' He indicated one of the profiles, which had somehow an unearthly, timeless quality of haunting sadness; light fell with melancholy upon the moulding of flesh and bone, upon the frozen movement of wind-tossed hair, and the hand resting on the shoulder echoed the eloquent line of the jaw. Together the half-face and the hand said everything that could be said about the loneliness of fame and the vulnerable nature of human beauty.

'Has Lensky the power to decide whether or not that's published?' Anna asked.

'He assumes what power he chooses. In that company he's God. A latter-day Diaghilev, you know — to whom, if one can believe all that one hears, Baran plays a somewhat stormy Nijinsky.'

'Oh.' Anna found that she did not want to pursue that idea. 'And you could fix for me to take some pictures of the company? And then, if they're any good, consider this book idea?'

'I'd say that was a sensible arrangement, wouldn't you?'

With a sense of giddy and faintly hysterical unbelief Anna agreed that this was a sensible arrangement, and tried to pretend to James Farmer and to herself that fate dropped such chances into her lap almost every day. He surprisingly enough seemed to be quite convinced by her display of sang-froid. He simply took for granted from that moment on that she was his colleague, so that in the end she herself had come to believe it and no longer found it absolutely terrifying, only rather like a waking dream.

2

James Farmer left Anna with the promise that he would be in touch with her as soon as the necessary arrangements with Lensky had been made. She then heard nothing from him for several days although she spent most of them in the flat in case he should ring, passing the time by turning her attention to redecorating. In a growing agony of suspense which came sometimes very near to rejection of the whole idea, she used up gallon after gallon of aubergine and white and scarlet emulsion, applying it with a concentrated ferocity she had not known one might summon to the painting of walls. The sitting-room was finished and the hall half so by the time the telephone at last rang and James Farmer's confident voice came at her over the line.

'Sorry it's been longer than I intended,' he had the grace to apologise. 'I had difficulty in getting hold of the great man.'

'Well, don't keep me in agony any longer!'

'Good lord, have you been worrying? No need for that — all's well, he likes the idea and the pictures of Baran, but he wants to meet you before absolutely committing himself.'

'Help!'

'Oh, I expected that, didn't you? I mean, you can't expect the poor dear to want just anyone tramping about his theatre with a camera.'

'But, James, what do I have to do? What does he want of me?'

'Just look as though you know your way around. Being pretty helps, of course.'

'Oh.' She wasn't sure whether or not this was a compliment, and, if it was, what she ought to say to it. He seemed, however, unconcerned with her response.

'I've told him we'll be at the theatre tonight,' he then devastatingly announced. 'I hope that doesn't disrupt your plans? I'll take you back to meet him after the show.'

'James!' Anna was deserted by speech, or by coherent thought. Dumbly she looked down at her paint-spattered and grubby bare feet, her multi-coloured hands; she knew that her long brown hair was lank and neglected and probably speckled with paint, too. And it was already half past four in the afternoon.

'It is a bit short notice.' He had the grace to sound a little shamefaced. 'But it was a case of catching him in a good mood, you see.'

'He sounds terrifying.'

'Oh, he is — but I'm assured by all the women I know that being terrified by Lensky is the most delicious experience, none of them would be without it. Don't take him too seriously. Seven-thirty tonight at your place, then? We can drink first and eat afterwards, if you'd like that. Oh, and we're dress circle, which means it.'

'Thank you,' she said rather limply, and when he had rung off stood helplessly by the telephone, a wet paintbrush still in her hand, and wondered how on earth she was to present herself in a fit state to grace the dress circle of the Imperial Theatre in virtually three hours' time. 'Serve him right,' she thought furiously, 'if I came like this!'

It was only somehow in a secondary way that the real importance of it dawned on her. It wasn't just an evening out with a charming but faintly unreal young man; it was her first excursion into that forbidden world behind the scenes of the ballet, it was a meeting with the impresario whose liking or disliking for the way she looked might decide everything in her future. It was — and she dared to think of it now for the first time — her first chance of meeting Alexei Baran. As the realisation of this came to her, Anna's stomach seemed to turn right over just once and then to grow very cold.

Trembling, she closed up the paint tin and went to put the brush into a jar of turps. The whole flat reeked of paint, but the sitting-room was now dramatic with aubergine walls, scarlet ceiling and white woodwork, and the hall began to look equally interesting. She seemed to see them for the first time, as though she had been painting them in a dream. She stood in the sitting-room and looked distractedly around her. What was she to wear? How to present herself so that Lensky, the great and terrifying Vladimir Lensky, should approve of what he saw and entrust her with the task of photographing his dancers?

In a panic she reviewed her wardrobe, certain that there was nothing in it fit to wear. Going to theatres on her own, she had not bothered to dress up, never sitting in the smarter parts of the house where it mattered; and in Midhampton there had never been any reason to do so. Vaguely she had thought of doing some shopping here sometime, but there had been so many other things to do, and no incentive to buy clothes. Now the inevitable crisis was upon her. Jeans, sweaters, shirts, one tweed suit, a few limp summer dresses, a trouser suit — nothing.

But there was a boutique a few streets away.

Hastily she scrubbed as much paint off herself as she could, and thrust her feet into comfortable old clogs and clattered away down the stairs, bag in hand, hot in pursuit of transformation. Half an hour later she was back, stumbling up the same steep and narrow stairs, past the importer's offices, past the mysterious milk-drinking Rodzinskas, panting up to her own front door under a small mountain of parcels, each of which represented a reckless plunge into the unknown.

It was all something of a gamble, she admitted to herself, having bathed, washed her long hair and brushed it almost dry, now trying on before her wardrobe mirror the clothes she had bought. Their effect on her apparent personality was astonishing. There was a brown silk jersey trouser suit which had first seduced her eye, sleek and clinging where it should, but falling loose and full at the wrist and below the knee. To go over it there was an ankle-length silvery beige mesh coat without sleeves, purely decorative. The girl in the boutique had pounced upon a pair of sand-coloured suede boots as being essential and absolutely right to complete the effect, and Anna had agreed. She had then fallen in love with a long, starkly simple black velvet kaftan buttoned with crystal at the neck and edged at the sleeves with black and silver braid. She had bought this, too, with velvet slippers to match. An agony of choice now faced her. Was it better to be warm and slightly earthy in brown silk or intensely dramatic in black velvet?

She considered herself in the mirror, trying to see herself with the eyes of a critical and possibly hostile stranger, a man of the world whose slightest whim in his own milieu was at once made law. Which version of Anna March, photographer, would he prefer to see? He was used to beautiful women; generally they were extremely thin beautiful women, being dancers, and built on a small scale. Anna wondered whether her own above-average height and her tendency to plumpness would in this case constitute an advantage. At least they made her different, though she had never before thought of them as potentially useful. Her height gave her a certain presence, and she had long ago trained herself to move with control and economy; otherwise she would have appeared coltish and clumsy, which she dreaded, normally trying to be as inconspicuous as possible. Tonight, suddenly, a sense of daring pervaded her. She was not any longer the Anna March of Midhampton days; she was a new creature, a Londoner, and she stood on the threshold of a world of music, of drama and glittering sophistication where to be as noticeable as possible was almost a duty. She wanted to impress the glossy James Farmer; she wanted Vladimir Lensky to look twice at her and to remember her. Of Baran it was better not to think.

Experimentally she drew up the thick mass of her long brown hair and twisted it into a knot at the crown of her head. At once the bones of her face seemed to take on a greater definition, the line of her jaw appeared finer and her neck long and smooth. Round her hazel eyes she smudged brown and yellowish colour so that the eyes themselves lit up with disconcerting flecks of marigold and yellow. The black kaftan, after this, was the only possible choice. It was devastating. When she had put it on she stared at her reflection in the wardrobe mirror, and did not know whether elation or cowardly terror was the more intense sensation.

Before she had time to lose courage or to change her mind James Farmer appeared, and was satisfactorily impressed.

'Lensky will fall stunned at your feet,' he assured her. 'You do look quite superb.'

'I was in a panic — it's all improvised at the eleventh hour, and Midhampton wouldn't recognise me.'

'Midhampton's loss is my gain, then. You don't look at all improvised, you look as though you probably wear diamonds in your bath.'

'Uncomfortable!' she protested, but laughed and was at ease with him. He was a companionable man; she began to feel that she might, after all, actually enjoy the evening if she could only forget for the time being about Lensky, forget her incredulity that all this could really be happening to her.

They strolled over to the theatre, along the narrow alleyway at the far side of it and round to the front, where light spilled out across the pavement and into the road. Taxis drew up to deposit their fares, the steps to the foyer were thronged with expensive, glittering people, there was a preponderance of furs, diamonds, long rustling skirts, and a great mingling of different perfumes in the air. Anna breathed it all in with a heady sense of mounting exhilaration. This was the way to go to the theatre; not, as she usually did, by the side door to the balcony, but in state, with a personable escort, mixing with people who looked as though what they did in the daytime might actually matter to the smooth running of the world.

James piloted her through the crimson-and-gold foyer, past photographs of the stars of the Imperial Ballet and up the Grand Stair towards the dress circle bar. Anna suddenly remembered the crate of empties in the flat, and accepted a gin and tonic with a feeling of slight reserve. However, the bar was clearly a meeting place for *habitués* of the ballet rather than of the bottle; glass in hand, James was launched on a tour of acquaintances among the crowd, and Anna found herself presented in swift succession to a bewildering number of people. Several of them were journalists or television people, names and faces that Anna knew well; she was slightly overwhelmed at being confronted with such celebrities as Carlos Martineau, conductor of the Philharmonic Symphony Orchestra, and his wife Helen, whose fame as a photographer put Anna much more in awe of her than of her husband. There was with them a little, middle-European man, faintly toad-like in appearance, with thick round glasses and teeth stained tobacco brown; Anna at first thought him quite repulsive, and then caught the eyes behind the thick lenses and found them shrewd, humorous and likeable. In all the gabble and laughter of the crowded bar she did not catch his name, but his personality lodged in her mind. Martineau himself was charming, a slight, wistful creature of deceptive mildness. His wife had a great deal of the grand manner, but Anna found herself attributing it to an unhappiness, a deep

40

discontent which she sensed in the woman, and could not understand how anyone so successful, with a husband like Martineau, could be other than pleased with life.

James seemed to know everyone who could lay claim to being anyone. To all of them he introduced Anna as 'a brilliant colleague of mine, a photographer', quite as though she were entirely established; she felt that she ought to be terrified of failing to live up to such a reputation, and yet could not help thoroughly enjoying being accepted by them as someone worth knowing — though, to be sure, Helen Martineau raised an eyebrow and said, 'A photographer?' in tones that clearly enough indicated her opinion of a supposed colleague whose name she had never before heard. The little European man seemed knowledgeable, however, and chatted amiably enough about the Lartigue and Cartier Bresson exhibition currently to be seen at the V. and A.

'Awfully good ones of Bradby's at the

Belman Galleries just now,' a rather exquisite person joined in from close by Anna's elbow. 'But he shouldn't attempt ballet — no sense of line or timing about his Blaise and Baran pictures, none at all.'

'But then,' said the little European man, 'who can photograph Baran if he won't co-operate? One knows the difficulties, alas.'

Anna remained silent, allowing James to introduce the newcomer, who proved to be the oddly named Simon Simon, a ballet critic whose column Anna read every Sunday in her newspaper. From the flowery character of his prose she had always suspected that he might run to velvet jackets and frilled cravats, and to her delight he did so, appearing beside the suave James positively tropical in magenta with cream lace.

'My dears, when did Baran ever co-operate with anyone?' Simon lamented now in plummy tones, looking agonised. 'But one forgives him. The law doesn't encompass divinity.'

'Divinity, on the other hand, might be expected to behave with a little more consideration,' murmured Carlos Martineau.

'Dear boy, don't be commonplace! Ah, but perhaps your good lady has crossed swords with him?' Simon turned limpid eyes upon Helen Martineau, who looked at him rather as though he were an infuriating blemish on an otherwise perfect negative.

'I consider my art to be quite as important as his,' she said bleakly. 'If he doesn't choose for me to photograph him, the loss is as much his as mine.'

'Too trying for you, Helen dear! But he does have this antipathy to all photographers, you know — not just to you.' He sounded positively to regret the impartiality of Baran's dislike. The little European man nodded his head.

'It's a curious phobia, in one so beautiful. But there is a deep magic about the making of an image, you know — in certain primitive tribes they believe that to own someone's likeness gives one power over his soul.'

'Baran,' said Helen Martineau, 'hasn't got a soul.'

'But such a *beautiful* body,' murmured Simon Simon sweetly, smiling at her.

Anna was rather glad that at that moment the five-minute buzzer sounded, breaking up the discussion and sending them severally in search of their seats. It wasn't any business of hers what the relationships between these people were, yet she felt fascinated, curious and a little alarmed — she, after all, had yet to attempt to photograph Baran officially. If Helen Martineau with all her beauty and brilliance had failed, what chance was there for the unknown and timorous Anna March from Midhampton? And it was obvious that a great deal of importance rested on the ability or otherwise to win Baran's favour.

Their seats were in the second row of the dress circle. Anna looked round her at the splendid dark crimson and gold auditorium and felt that for once she was part of the performance — a secondary performance, true, but one that contributed much to the total success of the evening. She wanted to print on her memory for ever, in case it should never be like this again, the richness and glitter, the jewelled sprays of light high above and the answering restless gleam of diamonds below, moving on wrists and ears as women bent and turned to speak, rustled programmes, lifted opera glasses. Usually all this was out of the range of her view from the balcony high above; one saw from there only the stage and a part of the orchestra pit, and a few boxes at the sides. Now she realised for the first time how lovely a theatre it was, baroque and elegant without tumbling over into fussiness; its proportions were exactly right, and it wore its gilded swags of fruit and flowers, its putti and its plaster drapery with the air of a woman who has decked herself for a grand occasion and knows that she looks well.

Tonight the air was distinctly festive. There were a great many flowers, banks of white carnations and red roses breathing soft perfume into the warm atmosphere. The royal box had in it at least one genuinely royal personage. In such an expensive and well dressed audience Anna felt surprisingly at home, knowing that she looked right, as unlike the Midhampton photographer as could possibly be. If this was a performance, then her part in it suited her very well.

Simon Simon was in the row behind them, and leaned forward to touch James on the shoulder just as the lights went down; what he had to say was lost in the applause for the conductor, and then the overture began, and Anna ceased to be interested in the audience, waiting instead for that magical moment when the great crimson curtain should part and be gathered up, and the familiar story begin, the old tale of the Sleeping Princess.

Vladimir Lensky's company had a very recognisable style, strong and lyrical in the great Kirov tradition. Gifted and musical dancers were drawn to it from all over the world. It was a modern version of the old Ballets Russe, and Lensky was its Diaghilev, the tyrant, magician, administrator and guide who welded together all the separate elements into a whole. Principal dancers of the Imperial Ballet were in their own world royal — and of those, Alexei Baran and Marcia Blaise were supreme. It was from them, from the mere fact of their dancing together, that tonight's sense of occasion sprang; there was always electricity in the air when Blaise and Baran danced. Anna sat motionless in the faintly rustling cavern of the darkened house, dimly aware of the spasmodic wink of jewellery caught by light from the stage, of profiles softly outlined, of the heavy perfume of carnations and roses; her attention was all on the glowing, brilliant hollow of the stage where the medieval figures of a fairy tale came to life, and the colour and the music, and the dramatic, stylised movements of the dance were an enchantment before which disbelief melted. Miracles of strength and balance and line were woven together into a corruscating pattern; impossible to believe that these were mere mortals, born with much the same physical endowments as oneself! Yet, for all their brilliance, it seemed a long time to wait for Blaise as the grown-up Aurora, and for Baran as her prince.

Princess Aurora's birthday came at last, and Blaise sparkled and glowed, the very essence of sixteen years old. She was, Anna knew, in real life all of forty-eight. Yet when she danced the role of a young girl, the shadow laid by time on her face lifted and she became a creature of fragile innocence, of freshness and vulnerability, her huge dark eyes full of the radiance of youth. It was all a matter of build and co-ordination, Anna told herself, determined not to be naïve; that, and talent, and then year upon year, hour after hour of unremitting, dedicated toil. That was all. No magic.

Blaise's first entry had set the air tingling. Now it was Baran's turn to be discovered, as fairy-tale princes so often are, hunting in a forest. He had a way of stalking on to the stage with so entire an assumption of authority that every eye at once turned to him; he dominated the scene merely by being there, and one could not for a moment ignore him. How daunting, Anna thought, for any ballerina to have to partner him if she were not absolutely confident of her own drawing-power. One might so easily be quite invisible beside him.

'Mark your prey,' James murmured in her ear. 'Still fancy the assignment?'

'Yes,' she admitted. 'Though it sounds even harder than I thought.'

'Watch Blaise. She has the knack of dealing with him.'

Anna hardly knew whether he was referring to the action on stage or to their private relationship. She watched as Prince Florimund followed his vision of the princess, led by the Lilac Fairy through the enchanted forest and into the cobwebby palace where sleep had reigned for a hundred years. There the sleeping Aurora wakened to his kiss and at once loved him. The thought came unbidden into Anna's head that here, surely, was every woman's secret dream. The old tale wrapped it all in symbol and mystery, but underneath them the meaning was very simple. What would it be like to be roused from the long sleep of girlhood by someone like Alexei Baran?

The lights came up for the interval, and Anna, ashamed of such mawkish flights of fancy, turned to James and began to enthuse about the dancing, Blaise's pure, perfect line, Baran's strength, elevation and musical intelligence. James let her babble on, looking at her rather oddly, agreeing with her

50

from time to time in an abstracted sort of way.

'One thing about these photos of yours, they'll certainly be passionate and committed,' he said at last, grinning at her. 'It's either going to be a wild success or the greatest disaster since the *Titanic* sank.'

'I'm only just beginning to feel any confidence. Don't kill it!'

'But I'll enjoy the whole thing either way,' he assured her, sounding as though he meant it.

The third act came then, leaving Anna no time to brood on what he had said. She thrust it to the back of her mind; useless to pretend that she wasn't involved or that she could be cool about it all, one couldn't be indifferent to Baran. Impossible now to resist the fire, the dazzle of the dances at Princess Aurora's wedding; she became as exhilarated, intoxicated as everyone else there, and at the end of it clapped until her palms burned. Through her opera glasses she examined the face that only a few days ago — though it seemed another lifetime — she had watched through a more powerful lens from the window of her flat. Ritually smiling, acknowledging the rapturous applause, Baran's face was a set, hollow mask of make-up, nothing behind it. The eyes, not smiling at all, glittered in the spotlight; black hair tumbled damply on to a brow beaded with perspiration. He held Marcia Blaise's hand in his, and when he turned to her Anna watched for some animation to liven his features, but none came, they remained fixed, smiling, empty. Petrushka, she thought; the sawdust puppet living only as the will of the cruel magician dictated. The Imperial Ballet was his St Petersburg fairground.

'A new game,' she murmured in James' ear. 'Hunt the missing dancer.'

'You find him elusive?'

'There's a mystery about him.'

'Doesn't exist,' said James decidedly. 'There's genuinely nothing to him. He's an attractive puppet.'

She was startled by his echo of what she had been thinking.

'That can't be so,' she insisted. 'No puppet could project so much feeling, such romantic intensity — '

'Oh, that's a trick — you'll soon discover it's so. The most stupid and shallow actor may on occasion wring the heart.'

'And the pictures I took? Was that a look of emptiness, of nothing?'

'Probably mulling over some unsatisfactory clause in his contract.'

'James!'

'I repent! I take it all back! No — I don't entirely believe the puppet theory. He's a genuine enigma. I offered merely one of the fashionable interpretations. Another is that he's loved Blaise ever since he met her six years ago, and is quietly dying of it.'

'Oh. And she?'

'Won't become involved with a boy young enough to be her son. There is the alternative theory, of course — that he's madly in love with Vladimir Lensky — '

'What rubbish!' she declared, trying not to blush. 'Any woman would tell you that's nonsense — he's very, very masculine.'

'Well, come and see what you think at close quarters.' James got to his feet. The curtain had come down for the last time, the house lights were up, and everyone around them had begun to move. People had in their eyes still a warm echo of the brilliance of the occasion; faces looked pleased and secretive, hugging their own memories.

Anna let James pilot her along the row and up the steps. The Martineaus and the little European man joined them from another row, and she heard James ask what they had thought.

'And what about you, Max?' he inquired of the little man, when the others had expressed themselves as delighted with the evening. 'Did it please your critical eye? Isn't it worth putting up with Baran to get some of what we've seen on film?'

Anna's heart jolted as though she had missed her footing. She blushed a sudden, fiery red, and dared not look back at them. She realised now who the little European man was, and why there had been something so elusively familiar about him. His name was Max Silbermann; she had seen pictures of him at the head of articles in the *National Journal* and other photographic magazines where he often wrote about aspects of his work. He was one of the great artists of the camera. He was also, rather astonishingly, the husband of Marcia Blaise.

3

On the other side of the pass door between the auditorium and backstage it was another world. Guided by James, Anna moved through confused impressions of dark corridors with cold stone floors and dingy painted walls, of rooms full of crates and hampers, of baize notice-boards stuck all over with lists and letters and telegrams. There was a great bustle and chatter, a coming and going of people of all kinds, scene-hands, dancers still in costume, busy little women in jumpers and skirts, and a number of men and women in evening dress strayed through from the auditorium and looking rather lost. Through one door for a moment Anna caught a glimpse of the great bare expanse of the stage, lit now only by a dingy working light and with all the flat board and canvas contrivance of the scenery exposed, shadowy and some-how shabby looking.

The room in which they finally came upon Vladimir Lensky was not at all what Anna had expected. It might have been the office of some administrator in a branch of local government, housed in temporary quarters; it was all desk, telephones, papers, hard wooden chairs, with lists, diagrams, plans fluttering from almost every inch of wall, and great steel filing cabinets frowning upon the untidy scene.

There were people in and out, congratulating, bringing messages, seeking instructions or merely calling good night. Lensky himself stood by a window which overlooked the side of the theatre and the stage door; with one hand he held the net curtain a little way open so that he could see the crowd beginning to form in the yellow lamplight alongside the building.

'The fools,' he commented flatly. 'The necessary fools. What do they gain by it?'

'A last glimpse into a world they long for. A closer look at their gods.' James was perfectly at ease in the man's presence; only Anna's heart seemed to have lost the even rhythm of its beating, making her breathless with uncertainty.

Lensky looked at them now as they stood just inside the doorway of his room. He was a very tall man, bearded, and rather heavy about the face and figure. He had a fine mane of dark hair, an acquiline nose, brilliant and commanding eyes. His hands, Anna thought, were the most beautiful thing about him, having very long, nervous, sensitive fingers, on one of which a great gold ring set with a black stone seemed a weight almost too heavy for the hand to carry.

He met her eyes now with a calculating, assessing look.

'The young lady who is to take pictures? So — ' He let fall the curtain and came forward, suddenly smooth and affable. 'Come here so that I may look at you, my dear.' Firm, dry fingers took and tilted her chin; the eyes that scrutinised her were unreadable, hard and black as obsidian. 'You are very young,' he said at last, when Anna could bear the gaze of those eyes no longer and pulled away from him.

'Does it matter?' she found herself saying, her heart beating so hard that it was difficult to speak steadily.

'You will disturb my dancers. You will fall in love with them, they with you.'

'Really!' she protested when she had got her breath back. 'That's hardly likely.'

'Your heart is already engaged?'

Not knowing what to say, she looked helplessly at James, and Lensky at once misread the look and exclaimed:

'Ah, I see! Then all may be well. And I congratulate you, Farmer, on your good fortune and your discernment. No — ' He lifted an imperious hand to stifle her protest. 'Say no more. I quite understand that you may think me too cautious, but — you see, my company is made of volatile stuff, my dancers are like precocious and difficult children. We cannot at the start of the season afford tensions, jealousies, scenes such as you might unwittingly cause.' He sighed, and suddenly, as though it tried his patience too far, dropped the flowery and elaborate manner and became entirely businesslike. 'What I mean, young lady, is this: I will tolerate your presence within my theatre so long as you are not in any way obtrusive and so long as you cause no trouble. But if you distract my dancers or impinge upon their work — out. And I give no second chances. Am I understood?'

'Perfectly,' she said through lips that felt cold and stiff. Something inside her stomach seemed to be frantically fluttering, otherwise she had gone quite numb with fright. James, sensing her helplessness, put a warm and reassuring hand under her elbow and gently squeezed, drawing her companionably to him.

'You're an ogre, Lensky,' he said, smiling. 'The girl has a talent quite as important as that of your dancers. She may well enhance what they have to give.'

'That is heresy, but I forgive you,' said Lensky magnificently. 'Besides, she is pretty. And I have seen the pictures of Alexei. They are good. I have promised them to Mannings of the *Sunday News* for the magazine next week.'

Anna felt as though the ground actually lurched beneath her feet. Wildly she stared at him, and could not for a moment make any sound, though she struggled for words.

'The *Sunday News*?' she at last got out, idiotically echoing him. 'Next week? But — '

'You don't mind, I'm sure?'

'Tremendous advance publicity,' James said close to her ear, reassuringly. 'And it'll do you a spot of good, too.'

'I — it's — I'm sorry, I'm just so astonished and — delighted. Yes, of course I am!' She tried to discover whether pleasure were anywhere to be found among all the riot of feelings

61

inside her; she could not be sure of it. Shock had jumbled everything and made any reasonable reaction impossible. 'Has — has *he* seen them?' she ventured. 'Baran, I mean?'

Lensky shook his head, lips pursed.

'I thought it best that he should not. We are, you know, not well disposed towards the camera.'

'Then he won't exactly feel kindly disposed towards me, will he? Didn't I once read that he attacked a press photographer?'

'He was provoked. Be a little circumspect, but don't worry. I will deal with any trouble of that kind.'

It was perhaps as well for Anna's courage that they were just then interrupted by a woman who came into the room, breathless and hurried, and stood on tiptoe to kiss Lensky on the cheek. She was not really the kind of person Anna would have thought likely to do that, a homely little thing in a plain black dress, with hair neatly plaited round her head — she looked as though her proper place might be in the wardrobe, or possibly behind a typewriter, someone's valued and long-trusted secretary.

'My dear,' Lensky said to her with astonishing gentleness, 'you have my thanks for tonight. It was very near perfection. And, look, here is someone new for you. I showed you those pictures of Alexei? This pretty creature took them, and promises to take some more.'

The woman turned on Anna a pair of huge eyes dark with the soft darkness of pansies, and Anna recognised her as Marcia Blaise.

'Miss Blaise!' she stammered, feeling horribly inadequate and foolish. 'I hadn't recognised you! Oh, but I loved tonight — you are so absolutely magical.'

'Thank you, really, thank you.' Marcia Blaise was smiling at her, genuinely pleased, a little spark of laughter warming her lovely eyes. 'People never do recognise me. It's a great blessing, I assure you. I did like your pictures of Alexei; are you going to photograph the rest of us soon?'

'I hope so. If I'm allowed — if I behave myself.' She suddenly found enough courage to look sidelong at Lensky, who smiled somewhat sardonically and said:

'Marcia knows well the rocks upon which the unwary may come to grief. She has seen it happen.'

'Oh, don't let him frighten you!' Marcia Blaise took and patted her hand. 'My husband's a photographer; he and Alexei haven't always seen eye to eye over what makes a good picture, but they've come to a certain understanding. I'm sure you'll reach one with Alexei, too.'

'Well,' said Lensky, 'come to class when you like, Miss March. You can discover times of rehearsal calls from the doorman. We shall see how you get on.' He turned to his desk as though suddenly tired of them, abruptly ending the interview. Marcia Blaise pulled a little wry face at Anna, and ushered them before her out into the corridor.

Once there she turned to James.

'We've not seen you for much too long. What have you been up to? We watched your TV play, and liked it, but that's the most we've seen of you for months.'

'Dear Marcia, I've been working. One does, you know, in secret and in silence.'

'You make it sound so noble and so spiritual.'

'Not very — a book about a critic who analyses everything, and finally himself, into a state of non-validity, and then, no longer able to justify his existence, dies.'

'How perfectly horrible! Yet I'm sure it will be marvellously funny to read.'

'Hilarious,' agreed James solemnly. 'We met up with Max before the show.'

'He's waiting in my dressing-room. Have supper with us? Dozens of people are going on to the Isadora.'

'Love to,' James said promptly. So it

was that they joined the party in Marcia Blaise's dressing-room, where Simon Simon was waiting with Max Silbermann and the Martineaus and a small constellation of other glittering names. But Alexei Baran was not among them. Despite everything, Anna felt disappointed, and then was angry with herself for daring to be so.

'Has Monseigneur yet made his exit?' someone was asking. 'Dare we go down?'

'Just going,' a man by the door informed them, looking along the corridor. Anna, being near enough to do so, looked out of the dressing-room, down the bare, shiny painted passage with its echoing floor. She was in time to see Baran depart, a superb dramatic figure in full-length furs, a black Cossack hat framing the perfect face that she seemed by now to know so well. He was accompanied by a small entourage, one of them staggering under a great burden of red roses. The procession turned towards the head of the stairs. Baran did not look back.

'Such thrills for the groupies!' a cynical voice muttered.

'One waits, it seems, for the circus to be over,' James murmured in Anna's ear. She turned to him, grateful for his presence, glad to be reminded that after all she wasn't dreaming. In all this extraordinary adventure he contrived to remain quite real.

'All right?' he asked her now. 'Not too much bemused?'

'I'm trying not to be. Does it show?'

'Not in the least. You are — though I don't suppose you're aware of it — being quite splendidly remote, calm and unassailable, as though you'd been wandering about these parts all your life.'

'I'm simply too scared to open my mouth.'

'Keep it up, then. You've practically made your name without having to pick up a camera.'

Throughout the rest of that extraordinary evening Anna kept reminding herself of what James had said, struggling to reassure herself, fighting a growing conviction that the whole incredible affair was a dream and that she would awaken soon to an empty flat, to be greeted by loneliness and silence. In a small fleet of taxis and cars the Blaise retinue moved off to the Isadora, where they were received like royalty, installed at a horseshoe of tables put together, and hovered over solicitously. Gradually, under the influence of good food and wine, and reassured by the way that she had been unquestioningly absorbed into the party, Anna began to forget her nerves and found that she was able to play the part written for her — for that was how it seemed, totally unreal, as though she were taking part in some extravagant play. She forgot to be in awe of Max Silbermann, and dared to tell him some at least of her dreams, her feelings about pictures and about her own work. She sat between him and James, feeling almost perfectly happy — only almost, because there would keep intruding upon her enjoyment the picture of Alexei Baran, furred and booted like a Tartar prince and going his own separate way. It had no reason to disturb her, but, unreasonably, it did so.

At some time in the early hours, Anna could not have said exactly when, the party finally broke up into scattered, glittering fragments in the darkness of the sleeping city. She remembered Marcia Blaise saying good night to her, saying to James, 'Take her safely home, we want to see her again soon.' She remembered Max Silbermann lifting her hand very gently to his lips, his eyes behind their thick spectacle lenses twinkling at her as though there were some delicious secret between the two of them. After that the taxi journey back to her flat was a blur; she assumed that James had got her up the stairs, that she had let herself into the flat and had fallen upon her bed fully dressed. She awoke at last from utter oblivion, to find that she was still in her black kaftan, clutching her evening bag, and that it was almost noon the next day.

James rang soon after she had surfaced, to inquire how she was feeling.

'Ghastly,' she confessed. 'I'm not used to drinking on that scale — or talking, for that matter. I think I got drunk on the conversation as much as anything.'

'You kept your end up very well. Marcia just rang to congratulate me on our engagement. She says I don't deserve you.'

'Our *engagement*? Oh, heavens — Lensky! I forgot — he misunderstood, didn't he, when I looked at you? — and you didn't correct him — '

'Because the misunderstanding seemed opportune. Do you very much dislike the idea of being vaguely supposed to be my property for the time being? We can easily break it off when it ceases to serve its purpose. But, you see, it would mean that Lensky is less inclined to suspect you of threatening the emotional lives of his dancers, wouldn't it? And that leaves you freer to work as you want.'

Anna's head seemed to be lurching about somewhere near the ceiling, rather like a balloon attached to her body by thin string. She was quite incapable of making any sensible or clear-sighted decision.

'James, whatever you think,' she said weakly, her eyes watering.

'Good! Splendid! Then we're engaged. I'll try not to take advantage, I promise.'

'But isn't anyone else going to object? I mean, there must be some girl — '

'I happen just now to be unnaturally free from all such snares and entanglements. Besides, this is business.'

'I know, but — oh, James, my head aches! What's best to take for a hangover?'

'Try hair of the dog. Failing that, I swear by Alka Seltzer, though they do fizz rather deafeningly.'

'I haven't any.'

'I'll bring you some.'

Surprisingly soon he was at the door, bearing Alka Seltzer and a bottle of wine. Anna, having bathed and changed into comfortingly familiar trousers and shirt, had begun to feel a little better.

'You were quick,' she said, and realised that she had never discovered where he lived. It seemed a strange thing not to know about one's fiancé.

'Russell Square,' he replied to her question. 'Handy for everything that matters. It's almost all University or offices now, but a few hardy residents linger on in the side streets. I like this part of London.'

'It's the only part I really know,' she told him. 'I've walked a lot of the rest, but only this area feels familiar.'

'Let's go for a walk, later. We can talk about the book, and I'll show you bits of Hyde Park and Kensington Gardens you never knew existed.'

This they did, once Anna was restored to something more like her normal self. James had come casually dressed in sweater and jeans today, rather as though he might have summed up Anna's probable wardrobe and come to the conclusion that such was her standard attire. She was relieved that nothing more in the way of high fashion was demanded of her. It was very simple to put on a long cardigan, comb her hair and set out with him. They made their way through Soho, and on through Mayfair, comfortably strolling, chatting about this and that, their past, their reactions to things they saw, to current ideas and trends. It was all pleasant and relaxed; Anna felt as though she were with a brother, or perhaps a friend of long standing, which struck her as being a disconcerting thing to feel about an almost unknown young man who had just constituted himself her fiancé — even though only in a temporary and impersonal capacity. She was bewildered by her feelings. He ought, surely, to flutter her heart just a little, to hasten the rate at which her pulse beat. He was

73

almost the first genuinely exciting man she had ever been out with — and yet he failed to excite her in any way. He felt instead as comfortable and ordinary as an old cardigan; she had the illusion of having known him a long time, and was sure that he held for her no element of mystery or surprise. She liked him without being greatly impressed. Feeling astonishingly blasé, she came to the conclusion that his polish, his air of having successfully interpreted all the best of the current trends, rather amused her. But he was good to have around, and his advent in her life had wrought such changes as she could scarcely have believed possible. She felt a little as though she had stepped on to a roller-coaster which had James at the controls; she trusted him, but wondered all the same whether he was really able now to stop what he had begun or even to influence its progress. She tried not to think of it, merely to go wherever events took her and make what capital she could of them, but it wasn't easy in so short a time to forget the caution she had learned over years.

'You really ought to have a ring,' James unexpectedly announced during their perambulation of Hyde Park.

'A ring?' She couldn't think what he meant.

'Engagement — remember?'

'Heavens, yes! I hadn't thought of that. Couldn't it be a modern, casual sort of engagement without a ring?'

'No,' he said firmly. 'I don't approve of so informal a way of doing things. What's more to the point, neither does Lensky. He'll expect to see you well and truly labelled. A nice clear warning to his dancers that you aren't available.'

So it was that Anna found herself in a jeweller's shop, confronting a tray of rings. In a sudden panic about James' money, she insisted that it must be a second-hand ring of no great value. With quiet determination James steered her in the direction of a lovely cluster of garnets and pearls.

'It suits you. It's the sort of ring you'd choose from preference, and verisimilitude matters, doesn't it? Lensky's no fool.'

Anna's sense of unreality increased. She accepted the ring rather as she might have accepted a doubtful tax rebate, with cautious pleasure.

'But of course it's yours,' she insisted. 'When we don't have to pretend any longer, I mean.'

'We'll see,' was all James would say. They left the vendor of the ring more than a little puzzled by the curious nature of their relationship.

On the way back to Anna's flat, James made more clear to her exactly what he wanted her to do with the projected book.

'I shall wait until you've exposed a film or two before I begin to shuffle words. I want you to look at the ballet with a new and entirely unprejudiced eye — forget Degas, forget everything you've ever seen before — just look, seek out what your eye finds. Make me wonder what kind of beings these are, who bend and extend their limbs into such tortuous postures — why do they do it? What do they want to convey? What is dance?'

She turned to him, not knowing whether to laugh or to cry.

'James, you make me afraid! A little provincial nobody, and you've pitched me into a world I've only ever dreamed of before. I have to keep telling myself — last night I had supper with Marcia Blaise and Max Silbermann, with the Martineaus, with Simon Simon — and I can't believe it! They treated me as an equal, and I know I'm not.'

The sun was behind his head, making a soft yellowish halo of his hair; his face, in shadow, was very gentle and understanding. He was, she realised then, quite a lot older than she had thought.

'Forget Midhampton, Anna,' he said. 'You aren't the same person. We all have to climb out of the great morass of our personal Midhampton if we have any talent and want to use it. This is your opportunity — grasp it! I had to do much the same myself, once.'

'You're successful enough now.'

'I make money and my name's known. That's not necessarily the same thing as success.'

For the first time she saw James as rather an impressive person. Perhaps, after all, she would find herself in love with him, gradually, not having been aware of the process. Was that perhaps the way love should happen? She had never been in love except in dreams, and did not know.

Passing the Imperial Theatre on the way back to the flat, Anna looked towards the stage door, remembering last night's crowds, the cheering when Marcia Blaise had walked with them out of the theatre. From that door now Alexei Baran abruptly came. Hands thrust deep in the pockets of his leather coat, a look on his face of black fury, he strode by them as though he did not see them and launched himself without pause into the stream of traffic noisily oozing along the street. Anna followed the rapid progress of his broad shoulders, his dark, arrogant head, across the bows of hooting taxis and on to the far pavement, where he disappeared from view down a narrow alleyway.

James shrugged his shoulders. Inside Anna, just under the place where her heart was, a curious, fluttering, clutching sensation began, as though a sudden sharp blow in the stomach had jolted the rhythm of her breathing. She stared after Baran, gazing blankly at the place where he had disappeared. She knew that if James had not been there she would have gone after him.

Dismayed, she contemplated the idiocy of such a reaction to the sight of the man, and refused to let herself pursue the thought any further. If she were to indulge in fantasy of this kind she might come to believe herself in love with him — and that would be the end of everything, she could not then pretend to James or to anyone else that she was a responsible adult in reasonable command of herself. That kind of love belonged to dreams; it was not for the daylight, ordinary world. It had nothing to do with real men and women.

All the same, she could not prevent herself from seeing suddenly that whatever she felt for James, it was nothing like romantic love. Nor could she entirely quell the restlessness in her, nor banish from her inward vision a haunting image of the dancer's unhappy face.

'Any lesser mortal would have been mown down by a bus,' commented James from far away. 'I wonder what's so much annoyed him.'

'It suits him to look that way,' Anna said, and was astonished to hear her own voice sounding quite steady. 'I'm sure he knows it. Come on — let's hurry home. I'm ready for some tea. We seem to have been walking for ever.'

4

Daily class was obligatory for dancers under contract to the Imperial. Whether it had been so or not, most of them would have gone to some class every day, since the suppleness which is vitally necessary to a dancer can only be maintained by constant, unremitting work.

It was held in the salon, a long room to one side of the theatre which had once been a foyer. Arriving a little before the ten o'clock start of the class, Anna was conducted by an amiable old man in carpet slippers and braces along a corridor painted pale green and spanning the back of the stage, up an abrupt flight of stone stairs, and into the salon.

Mirrors lined the walls, producing never-ending vistas of rooms diminishing into the distance. There were long blue curtains which could be drawn over them, Anna with some relief observed; there was otherwise something nightmarish about the unrelenting echoes of one's own image. A smooth wooden rail ran along each wall at about waist height. The floor was of very finely sanded wooden boards that shone like strips of satin. Across one corner of the room stood an upright piano with two chairs beside it; apart from that there was nothing in the room save for a tray of rosin on the floor just inside the doorway.

Anna moved cautiously forward, looking at her reflection in the mirrors and wishing that her nervous pallor did not so much betray her. She had put on her jeans and a knitted shirt, feeling that comfort and ease were more important than elegance, but now, seeing in her mind's eye the fragile and unsubstantial creatures who danced as though they had no weight, she felt that she looked large and lumpish, a great earthbound elephant strayed into a faery world. She wished that she had not to face them, that she could somehow take her pictures whilst herself remaining hidden.

The first comers were something of a shock to her. They wandered in through the door in twos and threes, chattering, rubbing together hands chilled by the crisp autumn air. They were dressed in the most extraordinary motley of old cardigans, sweaters, dingy and darned tights, with strange knitted stockings pulled on over the tights, or ribbed knee-mufflers, all looking somehow cutdown or second-hand, rather like the results of a mad forage at a jumble sale. Nor were they, seen close to, at all the aerial spirits of Anna's imagining. They were extremely muscular young men and women who walked with a flat-footed gait, toes turned out, every step they took making a very definite contact with the earth. They smiled at Anna as they saw her. They had beautiful faces, she thought; their faces quite made up for their muscular legs and curious attire. Seeing the camera that she had taken from her bag, one or two of them came over to speak to her.

'Lensky permits that you photograph?' one asked, her accent very Russian.

'Oh, you are brave!' another exclaimed. 'Maybe you have won the favour of Monseigneur?'

'*Taisez-vous!*' an Adonis-like young man admonished her from the *barre* where he was limbering up. 'You will frighten the lady. Then we shall *never* be featured in the colour supplements. Don't you *want* to be a household word?'

Another of the girls, a dark, doe-eyed creature somewhat slighter than the rest, was regarding Anna with an inexplicably mischievous and knowing look.

'You don't recognise me!' she reproached her in a small, husky voice with a faint accent.

'I'm sorry — should I? I can't remember — '

'But we live in the same house. My sister and I, we have the flat below yours. I am Nina Rodzinska.'

The milk-drinking Rodzinskas! Anna was filled with confusion, to think that they should know her when she had no idea of their identity.

'I've so often wondered who lived there,' she said, delighted that after all it should be someone so charming as this elfin little creature. 'I'd seen the name, but never a person to go with it.'

'We didn't know whether we should some time come and knock on your door. But you are never at home. You seem to be so busy, always going out with your camera.'

'Do come and knock on my door, any time, now that we've met. But give me time to answer, in case I'm shut in the dark-room. Does your sister dance, too?'

'No, Sonya is a translator. Sometimes she works for the B.B.C. When we travel abroad she comes with the company as interpreter. Listen — '

Nina touched her lightly, tentatively on the shoulder. 'Are you taking pictures for the Press?'

'No, they're for a book.'

'Ah — that's good. Maybe Monsiegneur will not mind. You have arranged with him?'

'You mean Lensky?'

'But no! I mean Baran.'

'Oh.' Anna's heart lurched. The hands that held the camera suddenly trembled. 'I think Lensky must have fixed it with him.'

'Oho! We shall see. All the same, don't let him bully you. The last one, he reduced to tears — it was *affroyant*!' Solemnly she nodded, as if to emphasise the horrific nature of the memory. Anna felt cold all over.

'I'm terrified,' she admitted miserably.

'Don't be so, then! He is after all not quite God. And then I think it would be good if someone for a change stood against him. For,' she said, and nodded again, wisely, 'it is not good for any man always to get his own way. He becomes out of touch with reality. And then he is no longer a very great dancer, but only a performing ape.'

The room had been filling up. Now, suddenly, a little, dumpy old woman was there among them, dressed in cardigan and slacks; her small face was white with powder and deeply wrinkled, like crumpled paper, her eyes small jet beads nestling among the folds. She clapped her hands, called, '*Silence! Allons — un, deux —* ' and as if by some conjurer's trick the class was at once lined up at the *barre* on two sides of the long room. A man seated at the piano began to thump out a rhythmical tune; backs straightened, knees and feet turned out, arms gently curved. As one the class dipped and rose with the beat of the music. Work had begun.

Hurriedly, Anna retreated to the corner by the piano, clutching her camera and light meter and bag, cursing herself for being caught unprepared and obvious in the middle of the room. She sank to the floor and sat there as unobtrusively as she could, studying the lines of dancers. No one took the slightest notice of her. For a few minutes she was entirely occupied by the effort of steadying the beating of her own heart, and could not begin to think coherently about what she was going to do next.

From her angle of view, seated upon the smooth wooden floor, the lines of legs lifting and falling with machine-like precision looked strange and beautiful, like some articulated geometric pattern. Only the occasional flicker of strain across a remote and beautiful face here or there betrayed the effort behind such gymnastic miracles. Insteps were haughtily arched, hands curved like melodic phrases from perfectly extended arms. Anna could see at once, even in these first few moments, along what lines her own work was going to develop.

She became oblivious of the ballet mistress with her darting black eyes which missed nothing; she ceased to hear the old, dried-up voice calling changes of step and position, or the relentlessly steady thump of the piano. It was as though she herself became a camera, searching out and framing whatever made a good picture. It was only after quite a long while, suddenly, that she found among all the beautiful faces the one she had photographed before. Baran was there in the class. He was half-way along the line at the left-hand *barre*, with Marcia Blaise just in front of him — she looked exactly as Anna had seen her in so many rehearsal photographs, all fine bone, huge eyes, delicate limbs. Baran had tied a band Apache-wise about his head, keeping back the long black hair and absorbing perspiration from a brow that looked already damp. They had all begun in varying degrees to perspire; it gave a shine to high cheekbones and smooth foreheads, accentuating the lovely structure of their faces.

Covertly she watched Baran, who seemed oblivious of everything but the strenuous efforts of his own body to describe perfection. From time to time the ballet mistress clapped to emphasise the beat, called it aloud, gave vent to fierce little cries of disapproval or command, entirely unimpressed by what she saw; perhaps there was some vision in her head of the peerless Maryinski in its greatest days, when Pavlova, Karsavina, Trefilova had flickered like living flames above its boards. Baran's face was utterly absorbed, as though there were no emotion in him, all dedication, determination. He must be one of the few great male dancers, Anna thought, who contrived to look perfectly proportioned, not over-developed in the chest and thighs. It was as though he had been designed expressly for what he did; dancing had not been thrust upon an ordinary body, distorting it, but instead this body had been intended, always, to dance. But was there anything of him besides the dancer? Even now, he did not look happy, only fiercely, passionately alive and utterly dedicated to the moment's gruelling task.

A brief pause, a hasty shedding of surplus cardigans, knee muffs, woollen tights, then the class went on, this time to more developed work on point, for which soft shoes were changed for those with blocked toes. Points, Anna discovered, made really an inordinate amount of noise on the smooth board floor. They supported real weight; no nonsense here about thistledown lightness. The effect of lightness came from balance and muscular control; so close to dancers at practice one saw the mechanism exposed, discovering the real physical effort, the superb training and discipline which produced the illusion. For the men point work was modified, their function now being to lift and support, for which strength rather than fine balance must be fostered. They retained soft shoes and adapted what of the women's steps were applicable. The piano thumped on, emphasising the beat less, the music now a little more varied and melodic. Anna sat and absorbed everything. The camera lay unheeded in her lap, not exactly forgotten, but not so far of any use. She would take pictures on film tomorrow; today her eyes worked for her, selecting and planning. After this she would know exactly what to do.

The class came to an end, the godlike and super-human creatures became exhausted, perspiring human beings, somehow shrunken in stature, a motley, rag-bag crew in their assorted leotards and darned tights, the hair damp around their temples. Anna tried to watch Baran without appearing to watch him. He turned to Marcia Blaise and took her hand, pressing it to his lips; he bowed briefly to the ballet mistress, and then strode out of the room, looking neither to left nor to right, as though there had been simply no one else there. Blaise for a moment looked after him, and on her small oval face a confusion of expressions struggled, regret and a kind of yearning visible among them.

People obscured Anna's vision then. A little stiffly she got to her feet, clutching her camera, meter and bag. She felt as though she had been deeply asleep. Nina Rodzinska appeared suddenly before her.

'You took no photographs! I listen for the click, I look for the camera — but nothing! Are we not beautiful?'

'So beautiful that I forgot to take pictures, I was so lost in gazing. No — really, I'll take some tomorrow. Today I was thinking about how to approach it and what to show.'

'How very intellectual you are!' Nina was teasing; her lovely, pointed face looked cat-like, alive with mischief. 'Come,' she went on, 'have you more to do here? Or will you come home with me? It would be nice to talk, and we can have coffee — even a cake, for once, though I shall feel evil for the rest of the day.'

'I'd love to come. Do you have to diet? You look so fragile — '

'Oh, we all diet, all of the time. A *bêtise*, but necessary.' The girl was shrugging on an ancient grey cardigan which zipped up at the front; she had a small soft-topped case with her, from which she produced a pair of trousers, stepping into them and at once looking in some extraordinary, inexplicable way extremely fashionable. Her shoes were swiftly exchanged for bright yellow clogs, and she was ready to leave. Anna watched the transformation in astonishment.

'It's quicker than the dressing-room,' Nina explained. 'That's along miles of cold corridors. And I only have to walk round the theatre and across the road — I can change properly at home.'

There were others doing the same quick change. Most of the men, however, had gone, towels draped about them, to shower and to change more thoroughly. The man from the piano had disappeared; the ballet mistress was talking to Marcia Blaise, who now swiftly kissed the old woman's hand

and pressed it momentarily to her cheek, and then turned away from her, and saw Anna.

'Hello,' she said, smiling and coming over to her, genuinely pleased to see her. 'How are you? And James, after our little party?'

'It was a lovely party — it took us most of yesterday to recover, but it was worth it.'

'We're so pleased about you and James. Now we can stop nagging him about its being time he found someone nice and settled down.'

Guilt made Anna blush. She would have to get used to being James' fiancée, but it was easier to talk about in the abstract than to do in fact. She still could not reconcile herself to deception.

'We'll see you this afternoon, perhaps?' Marcia Blaise asked. 'There's a full call at two-thirty for *Les Sylphides* — in dress, too, so you should get some good shots, I should think.'

'That sounds marvellous. Yes, I'll come.'

Blaise left them then, with a little, affectionate touch on the cheek for Nina, who blushed and seemed somehow to flower under the warmth of the gesture.

'They call her the First Lady,' she said. 'It's her due, don't you think? So many of them would never even notice a mere choryphée. But she — '

'I think she's one of the sweetest people I've ever met,' said Anna. 'But I find it hard to believe that it's true, that I have met her and count as one of her friends.'

'Tell me about James,' demanded Nina, linking arms with her and making for the door. 'Is it our James Farmer from upstairs? Are you engaged to marry him?'

Anna admitted to a fiancé who had once lived in the flat she now occupied.

'Of course, you must know him,' she said to Nina.

'Alas, not well enough. We admired him from a distance. But soon after we came to live in our flat he moved away, so we never got to know him as we had planned to do. Also,' she pointed out, 'since he must then have been in love with you it would have done us no good. *C'est la vie!*'

Anna felt more than ever guilty and unsure of being able to uphold the deception. She accompanied Nina from the theatre, walking in the little dancer's wake as she went rapidly out of the stage door, waved to the doorman in his cubby-hole just inside the doorway, and set off at a great pace round the theatre. 'You shall tell me everything about the fascinating James,' she was saying as she went. 'And I will tell you the scandal of my world. It will be very satisfactory.'

It was, in a way. Over very good coffee in the milk-drinking Rodzinskas' cheerful, cluttered and haphazard kitchen, Anna learned a great many things about the Imperial Ballet. There was a very strong family feeling in the company, to which Lensky was a kind of remote father, an absolute autocrat whose word on the lightest of subjects was law. He was jealous of his dancers, strict about their daily lives; for instance, he expected of them early nights even when they were not dancing, and was quick to pounce on the least sign of listlessness or strain. They were not encouraged to marry — certainly not if they had any real promise of brilliance; but if despite him they insisted on their right to do so, the chosen partner must be approved by *le Maître*, or dire displeasure would be incurred and a contract probably ended.

'And that, my dear, is death!' Nina pulled a wry face. 'There are too many dancers in the world.'

'Surely not all of the Imperial's standard?'

'Oh, well — but it's not easy to leap from one company to another, especially if you have been dismissed by a man like Lensky — ' She shrugged, a graceful, expressive little movement. She had showered, and was wrapped now from head to foot in a white towelling robe, looking more than ever like a soft little white cat. Anna felt florid and strapping beside her, and yet could not resent it; it seemed somehow to be the natural order of things. Almost anyone would have appeared too large at the side of Nina.

'There's a rumour that someone took some wonderful but daring photographs of Monseigneur,' Nina went on. 'Was it you? Is that how you come into the picture?'

'I did take some. He was standing on that little balcony — above the staircase block, you know, across the road from here. He wasn't being anyone, or pretending — just looking very lost and unhappy.'

'So you photographed him? That was — brave. He does not yet know.'

'When he does — ?'

'*Boum!*' Nina made a wide, explosive gesture, her eyes huge and horrified. 'You will do well to hide. He almost pathologically hates to be photographed. Once, you know, he seized a camera and smashed it to smithereens on the ground. And once he seized a photographer — such excitement! The poor man sued, but didn't win.'

'Why does he do it?' Anna demanded, determined not to be frightened, sure that if she once understood the cause of his behaviour she would be able to circumvent it and escape unscathed. Her heart was beating too rapidly, not from fear but from the very thought of Baran himself, which filled her with agitation.

'Oh,' said Nina, 'who knows? He feels, I think, that the camera pries — that somehow, I don't know — that it attacks him, that it is a horrid, peering eye searching out weakness, seeking something for the crowd to laugh at. And then, you know, he adores the First Lady — they say that he has passionately loved her since he first saw her dance when she visited Leningrad, and that he came to the West to be near her — and, you see, her husband is a photographer.'

'A very great photographer,' Anna said. 'And the dearest little man — but a surprising person for Blaise to have married, all the same.'

'They are very fond. She feels some *tendresse* for Monseigneur, I am sure, but — no one really knows, though they say that she keeps him at a distance and that he breaks his heart for her.'

'How sad, Nina — how really, terribly sad, if it's true.'

'*If* it's true.' Nina made a wry grimace. 'They will say anything, the gossips — you will find the company, and the hangers-on, full of many spiteful stories. Don't believe them all. Like any family, we quarrel — and being of the theatre, and then many of us at least half-Russian — well, need I say more? You understand.'

Anna hoped that she did. But it was all so much a world of books, of films, of dreams; there was nothing recognisably the same as it would be in Midhampton. Sometimes she felt as though she were talking, parrot-fashion, a language she did not really know. In Midhampton men did not die for love of women old enough to be their mothers. But then, in Midhampton no such men and no such women as Baran and Blaise existed. Midhampton did not even have a theatre.

'Of course,' Nina went on calmly, 'it is all much complicated by Volodya Lensky, who himself loves Monseigneur and is very jealous. It would not so much matter if he were not passionately devoted to the ballet — for, you see, he must recognise Blaise's supreme gifts, he must have her dance in his company and partner Baran, for they are made for each other. It torments him — but together they are gods, you agree?'

'Oh, I agree,' said Anna faintly. Neither could Midhampton have produced this variation. She felt dizzy; the dream seemed to have taken on darker tones, and she was trapped in it. She watched Nina move from the table to the cooker where there was coffee still in the pot. The girl looked innocent and fresh as a nun in her white robe. How could one live in such an atmosphere as that at the Imperial and look still so untouched?

'You are shocked,' Nina said, pouring coffee, her back to Anna. 'I am sorry — I shouldn't retail the gossip, should I? Especially as it probably isn't true.'

'Surely you know if it's true or not?'

'One sees little moments, you know — little glimpses of what may be going on. But they are very far above us, the principals — and Lensky, he is God.'

'But they come to class.'

'Everyone comes to class. But that is not to say that we mingle. Monseigneur doesn't know that I exist. The First Lady is an exception; she is so far above us that she can ignore the rules and mix with the mortals. It is part of her charm that she does so.'

But Anna, going back with Nina into the theatre for the afternoon's stage rehearsal, carried with her a new picture of the company, in which dark and elemental passions lay uneasily contained under a veneer of artistic dedication. She had seen them until now as artists existing primarily for the dance, taking their identity from it. Baran's face in the pictures she had taken had opened up other possibilities; he had become a person to her — still remote, still mysterious, but recognisably human and disturbing to her as a man. Now, quite suddenly, there came upon her the understanding that of course they were first of all people who happened to be also dancers; they had lives of emotion and passion quite outside of the unremitting structure of a dancer's life. One might be dedicated to the dance and yet break one's heart for love.

She had wanted to be able to admire them, even to love them, without fear of disillusionment — that was the reason for her limited and unrealistic view of them, she realised. She had wanted it safe and tidy. But it wasn't; like all life, the theatre and the dance were vulnerable to people's private obsessions. Oddly enough, having come to this understanding, Anna began to feel much better. Her sense of unreality faded; she no longer felt that she moved among gods, but saw them as people not much different from herself, and felt that she had an identity of her own among them.

She found her way on to the stage, trying not to get in the way of any of the people dodging about behind the wooden flats and wandering on and off the stage. There were scene-shifters, electricians, wardrobe women, dancers already in costume; the stage was lit, a moonlit grove of trees with a dark stone ruin at the back, all ivy-hung and impossibly romantic — *Les Sylphides* being that kind of a ballet. Anna took light readings and then stationed herself behind a flat whose edge was fretted with leaf shapes. The props and weights supporting it got rather in her way, but she felt too shy to place herself any more prominently. As it was, she had an interesting sidelong view of the stage. Later she would see if she could go into the orchestra pit and get something from there, or even get round the proscenium arch where she would be out of the way and yet have a superb view. Plenty of time for that; there would be other rehearsals. This was just a beginning.

It seemed to be a full dress rehearsal with orchestra. The dancers now were all ethereal in long filmy tutus and chaplets of flowers. The music sounded very distant from Anna's place in the wings, echoing hollowly round the dark, empty house. She listened to the graceful, melancholy-romantic phrases, and watched the groupings and re-groupings of stately, gauzy figures on the stage, and did not realise until he stalked past her into the lights that she had chosen to stand exactly where the Poet, Baran, made his first entrance. He had gone past her in a moment and was received at once into the strange faery world of Sylphides, their white arms beckoning and ensnaring him. But in that moment of passing he had seen her camera; Anna had felt a flash of anger strike like lightning from his eyes, and knew that there would unavoidably, sometime, be a storm.

5

To Anna's surprise, Baran came off stage at the end of his first solo without taking any notice of her. She had already used up film at a feverish rate, fearing that she might be banished once he had had a chance to complain about her presence. There were, she knew, some lovely shots of frozen arabesques and clusters of white tutus like mist against the light, of swan necks and beautiful faces, of Baran himself, caught in the air, in that one still moment at the top of a leap when he seemed to rest suspended as though he could somehow by an effort of will neutralise the pull of gravity. The brilliant lights emphasised features so that faces looked curiously masklike save for the glitter of the eyes. They were all unreal creatures out of a poet's dream.

Since no one disturbed her, and Baran came nowhere near her again, Anna continued with her work, forgetting in her absorption that she had any cause for apprehension. She must, after all, have mistaken that flash of his eyes as he passed by the first time. It had been the light catching them; his tension had been born of the demands of dancing.

It came therefore as all the more of a shock when, as the last lovely tableau froze into immobility, as the lingering strains of the music died away, Baran dropped suddenly out of the role of romantic poet, strode purposefully to the side of the stage, and, before she had realised what he was going to do, seized Anna by the wrist and dragged her out of hiding.

Lights blazed down on her, blinding her eyes, dazzling and confusing her; she could feel the heat of them on her skin. Baran hauled her downstage, making nothing of her instinctive, panic-stricken resistance. Hard, hot fingers were like a tight manacle about her wrist; she felt as though if she struggled she might break her bones before she broke that grip. With her one free hand she desperately tried to secure the camera, the spare lens and cassette she had been holding; she turned her head aside from the blinding flare of the lights. Behind her the lovely group of white Sylphides had broken up into separate, immobile figures, tensely watching; she felt the sympathetic fear with which they were holding their breath, waiting for the catastrophe.

'And what — ' demanded Alexei Baran dangerously into the great void beyond the lights, ' — what is this that I find in the wings? I do not remember giving my permission for photographs. I do not even remember that my consent was asked.'

'I, nevertheless, have given it,' came Vladimir Lensky's languid, clear drawl out of the darkness. Anna began to be able to see something of the theatre, the gilded plaster putti and flowers glinting on the front of the circle, the rows of crimson seats standing empty. She saw that Lensky had risen from a place in the stalls and was sauntering down towards the rail round the orchestra pit, his attitude expressive of faint boredom.

She looked at Baran, only now comprehending that it was he, his hand round her wrist, his powerful, compact body inches from her own. His face was a mask in which the grey eyes burned with cold fury, and his breath came rapidly with anger. Anna began to tremble.

'My consent is not yours to give, Vladimir Ivanovitch,' the dancer said now, his voice terrifyingly soft and charged with fury. 'I dance Petrushka only so often as it is specified in my contract. I am not otherwise your puppet. This I will *not* take!' and Anna was shaken like a rag doll.

'My dear Alyosha, calm yourself. This young lady is not of the Press — she takes pictures in which there is much distinction. They may even flatter us all. She is here at my invitation.'

Baran now for the first time turned his gaze on Anna. The eyes burned, the nostrils flared — he looked angry beyond reason, utterly without compassion, an imperious and totally selfish autocrat whose will had been crossed. Again, contemptuously, he shook her, bruising her wrist until the bones felt as though they must splinter. He seemed not to hear her involuntary cry of pain.

'What has this — this creature to contribute to *my* art?' he demanded. 'And even if she could, why was I not asked? You insult me, Lensky. I will not be insulted!' With a movement so swift that she could do nothing to prevent it, he snatched suddenly at the camera, released Anna, and lifted the camera high above his head before smashing it with all his enormous strength on to the stage. It shattered there like a small bomb into several pieces, which shot in all directions.

For a moment Anna was too

stunned, too paralysed by shock to do anything. She looked dumbly at the wreckage of her camera, still scattering, still rolling down the slope of the stage. A cry of rage, a raw, inarticulate yell, suddenly burst from her, and as though that released some deep spring within her she leapt at Baran, blindly hitting out at him, clutching at his hair; her fingers found a hold and she hung on, pulling down his head and lashing out at it with her other fist. For a moment he staggered under the attack, and then, recovering from surprise — for clearly he was not used to retaliation from his victims — he seized her by the waist, lifted her clear of the boards and tossed her away from him as though she had no weight at all. Still grasping a sparse handful of curling black hair, Anna staggered back and fell. Baran turned and stalked from the stage, leaving it shattered like a battlefield behind him.

There was a moment's stunned silence, and then, with little, horrified, compassionate cries, the dancers still onstage pattered forward in their satin point shoes, settling round Anna like a cloud of swansdown, lovely faces peering down at her in concern and white hands reaching out to help her. With a presence of mind that astonished her she warned them:

'Please look out for the film cassette — it's probably rolled somewhere, and I don't want to lose that, too.'

'Are you all right, Anna?' It was Marcia Blaise who spoke, coming through the crowd to kneel beside her, the choryphées clustering around her like attendant spirits, quite unconsciously grouping themselves in a charming tableau. Anna was filled with giddy and inappropriate laughter; she was shaken into it, as one sometimes is by shock, and found herself helplessly giggling.

'Yes, really — I'm much more shaken than hurt. I've never been hit by an Olympian thunderbolt before!'

'One cannot apologise for him,'

Marcia Blaise said. Her small face was white and angry, and very unhappy. 'He will apologise, I promise you. All the same — ' 'Miss March,' Lensky's accented drawl interrupted them, 'I did not think that this would happen.' The group of dancers parted to let him through. 'I am very sorry. You are not hurt, I hope?'

'In nothing more than my *amour propre*,' she said, her hysteria subsiding. There was genuine approval in his smile, and warmth in his hands steadying her as she got to her feet.

'We shall put matters right,' he said reassuringly. 'First you will buy yourself a new camera and charge it to me. And this moment I think you need a drink. Come with me, we will find something to restore your confidence.' He put an arm round her shoulders, contriving to do so in some curiously formal and impersonal way as though he conferred on her a unique honour. The choryphées again moved back, forming a strange little guard of honour across the stage; one of them held out her hand to Anna, displaying the missing film cassette.

'Oh, thank you — that's marvellous!' Anna was enormously relieved and pleased. Baran after all had made this dramatic and rather childish fuss to no effect; she had almost all of the film she had shot quite safe. And Lensky was on her side — everyone was on her side. The incident had merely won sympathy for her.

She became suddenly conscious of her bruises, which ached and set her trembling. Lensky hurried her off the stage, hastily dismissing the company, directing the wizened old ballet mistress, waiting in the wings, to go after them: 'Tell Vassya, in the Nocturne, not too much *élevé* — and Milanova must watch the beat, she is not always *ensemble* today — otherwise OK, I think.'

He led Anna to his room, and there from a cupboard produced a brandy bottle and glasses.

'You drink — then we talk a little.'

'Thank you.' Gratefully, Anna obeyed him, feeling chilled and oddly loose in the joints as though if she had to move now she might begin to fall apart. Baran's scornful face had begun to burn so bright in her memory that it obscured everything else. The numbness of shock was wearing off. She sat heavily down on the chair Lensky brought forward for her. He himself took his seat at the desk and regarded her across it, a certain calculation even now underlying the concern and sympathy in his eyes.

'There are great pressures on him,' he abruptly stated. 'You understand?'

'No — not really. After all, there are pressures on all of us from time to time. I don't find my job easy.'

The fall must have scrambled and rearranged her wits, she thought; she was not normally so crisp in the face of disaster. Not the Midhampton Anna March, certainly. But then . . .

'But for Baran, everything is magnified by the lights, the loneliness. The

117

camera lens magnifies — he hates to be pinned out for dissection in the Press, even though for the sake of publicity he must sometimes endure it. He is very solitary. He suffers all that he suffers alone and in silence; he does not know how to trust or to share.'

'Why not?'

'He was never taught. He was not loved, as a child. They sent him to ballet school to get him out of the way, merely — did you not know that? And they never pretended to him that it was otherwise.'

'Were they so poor?'

'On the contrary — they were comparatively rich. Both intellectuals, both scientists high in the Soviet world — but with no room for a child in their lives. He showed aptitude for the dance, and so they gave him the dance to love. In that he has had to find all his emotional satisfaction. I speak,' added Lensky somewhat belatedly, 'in confidence. It is between the two of us.'

'Naturally.'

'For him, as for all great artists, there is tension when the emotional balance is disturbed. Of late there have been problems. I know that my company — my children — consider me cold, Miss March. They think that I have no understanding, no sympathy for the affairs of the heart. How they are mistaken! It is just because I do understand how distracting, how painful and also how impermanent are these affairs that I discourage them. To dance — really to dance — one must love nothing, no one, better than the dance. It's simple. But for a great dancer such as Baran, not always easy.'

'One gets the impression that he loves himself above all.'

'No. First the dance — then himself. Then — ' Lensky shrugged. 'There is much pressure within him, much pain. Forgive him, my dear. You have so much that he can never have. You can afford to be charitable.'

'Since he hurt only my camera, and you have promised me another — ' She smiled at him, but felt the smile not reaching her eyes; inside she was still shaken and cold, and sometime would need to cry.

'The film was saved?' Lensky asked.

'Yes — two cassettes of it, this one and another in my bag. I'd only just started on the third film, only a few frames have been spoiled.'

'Print the films and let me see them. If they are good, I will show them to Alexei. That way we may placate him.'

'Has he — has he yet seen the other ones I took of him?'

'No. I think best not to tell him. He might cause trouble with the newspaper. He must not think that he can dictate to me — this is my company, and I run it as I think fit. I,' said Lensky magnificently, 'intend to have my way. Then, if he must sulk — well — !' He shrugged, dismissing the matter. To Anna, this dealing with people as though their own wishes were of no account seemed cold-blooded, arrogant, but she tried to remember that

Lensky was an autocrat in his own world, and that his world was one not bound by the normal rules.

She felt better for the brandy, and was able to get up now to take her leave of him quite steadily, as though nothing had happened.

'I must go and develop the films, if you want to see them.'

'Drop them in at the theatre door if you can't find me. We are still friends, Miss March? You aren't angry with me?'

'Oh, I'd never blame the zoo-keeper if one of his lions bit me. It's the nature of the beast, after all.' She felt that it was a reasonably good exit line, all things considered. Lensky seemed to appreciate it.

She had to go back to the stage to get her camera bag, which still stood in the deep shadow of the flat where she had left it. The stage was almost dark now, lit by a dim reflected glow from the auditorium. In the great towering space above the stage a dense hanging forest of wood and canvas very gently sighed and fractionally swayed in the almost imperceptible currents of air. Everything else seemed very still. The forest glade with its romantic ruin had sunk into gloom, two-dimensional and unreal without its necessary lighting. Everyone had gone to tea, leaving only the deserted shell of the dream that had lived there. It was strange and eerie, and rather sad.

She took her bag, and hurried away from the darkened wings, back into the normal echoing bustle of the corridors, and then out of the stage door. She wished that she could find Nina, but did not know where to look for her and dared not go exploring in case she should bump into Baran himself. What her reaction to meeting him would be she did not know, but shrank from the thought of it; where his image had been in her mind there was now a great pain which she could not bear yet to examine.

A woman's voice called her as she

began to walk away. Turning, she saw Marcia Blaise coming after her, a small, very nearly insignificant figure again in jumper and skirt with an old mackintosh pulled anyhow over them.

'Anna, I must have a word with you, just for a moment.'

'Of course.' Anna smiled, wanting to reassure her. Everything else in her head might be in a terrible muddle, but she was entirely clear about not wanting to have upset the First Lady, feeling that of all the people she had met at the Imperial this was the most deserving of the crowd's adulation.

'Anna, dear — ' Blaise put a gentle, almost timorous hand on her arm; the great dark eyes were unhappy. 'I wanted a little to explain, if I could — so that you might forgive him. I — feel some responsibility — '

'But you mustn't, surely — '

'He is so unhappy! I have failed him, Anna — not in any way that I can explain, not in the obvious way — oh, there's no accounting for it! I know it's hard, but one must make allowances. And Lensky is a fool not to have told him you were coming. He deals with him in quite the wrong way.'

'I do understand. I know there are pressures on Baran. You saw the photos I took the other day? Well, then — they spoke clearly enough, didn't they? I won't bear a grudge. But I do intend to work with the company, whether he likes it or not.' She trembled as she said it, but meant it, stubborn as she had rarely been in the whole of her life. She would not now be forced by anyone to let go her hold on the reality of her dream.

'That is absolutely understood,' the older woman said, and squeezed her arm. 'Go and tell James all about it. He'll think it no end of a story! Give him my love.'

'I will.' It confused Anna to have to return to the fiction of James the fiancé. Aching and dispirited, she made her way round the theatre and across Bloom Street, thinking that she must ring James at once and tell him what had happened. But there was no need. She turned up the last flight of stairs to her flat and found James and Nina sitting side by side on the top step, Nina in full verbal spate, and James listening with an expression of mingled horror and delight.

'Anna!' He leapt to his feet and took her hands in his, as concerned and solicitous as any fiancé might be expected to be. 'Poor old thing, you did go in at the deep end! Are you all right?'

'Yes — I'm all right.' She quelled a sudden, foolish desire to burst into tears. Delayed shock, she thought detachedly, producing her key and letting them all into the flat. 'I'd like a cup of tea, though — and something to eat. I'm starving!'

'Pronto,' James declared, heading for the kitchen. He was a dear, Anna thought; really, he would be very nice to be engaged to in fact, and not just in the course of this charade. The whole business of the fake engagement, the allaying of Lensky's fears, looked suddenly grotesque and unnecessary. She felt a strong urge to tell Nina the truth, to explode the fantastic situation and settle for reality. But that, too, must be the result of shock — she wasn't reliable just now on any subject involving her own emotions.

'You were absolutely *magnifique!*' Nina earnestly assured her, going with her into the sitting-room where she dumped her camera case. 'Everyone was entirely for you — you will come and take more photos?'

'Certainly. I don't intend to be put off by one man's tantrums.'

'Temperament!' admonished Nina, shocked. 'You must call it temperament, not tantrums — so like the nursery — '

'Behaviour that belongs in the nursery deserves a nursery word. So far as I'm concerned, Baran threw a nasty little tantrum. He's a bully, and bullies mustn't be encouraged to think that they can always get away with it.'

'But he is a genius — and truly unhappy. It is the theatre, *ma chérie* — remember always that in the theatre, or maybe only in the ballet, and *Russes*, as we are — temperaments are exaggerated, explosive. We act a little all the time. Allow for that.'

'Oh, I suppose I must.' Wearily, Anna flopped down on to one of the granule sacks, which sagged awkwardly under her. 'Damn these things! I must get some furniture.'

'But the room is beautiful — so strange, so challenging!' Nina looked round her at the aubergine walls, the scarlet ceiling, the white window-frames and box shelves. Even the brown lino somehow contrived to appear right. It was a good room, Anna decided, seeing it anew. There were certain settled things that had come right in her life, and this was one of them.

'You are fortunate, you know,' Nina said now, as though she read Anna's thoughts. 'You have this nice flat — and you have James.'

'Don't you have anyone, Nina? There were some very handsome young men in class this morning.'

'Alas,' lamented Nina, 'Lensky, he is hard. We are not permitted to fall in love. It isn't *quite* written into our contracts, but — '

'Of course, you told me. All the same, how can you help it? Love happens, surely, like — like catching a cold. You can't avoid it.' She thought of her own strange compulsion towards Baran. Could that be what was meant by the word 'love'?

'Darling, you do put things so romantically!' Nina protested. 'But I understand. We try to avoid the possibility of infection, I suppose you would say — if we care about our work enough. We work hard, we lead little social life, we — ah, if need be we contrive the small *affaire* which does not mean too much.' Nina shrugged. It was extraordinary, to hear so cynical an exposition from such a flower-fresh creature. 'One knows that Lensky demands this,' she continued. 'It's a measure of one's love of the ballet that one accepts it. If a girl — or a boy — wants to be free to love, then she or he must not hope to dance with the Imperial company. It's a choice one must make.'

'I'd have thought all that quite out of date — I thought the concept of total dedication died with Diaghilev. Surely one can fall in love and dance well?'

'Maybe you are right. It depends — on the spirit that is in the company, among other things. And then, how much of oneself — dreams, ambition, time, passion — one gives to the dance. To get absolutely to the top, like Blaise and Baran, one must have first the talent from God, and then the ruthless, single mind. No room for any other great love.'

'Blaise is married.'

'You know him? Well, then — ' She spread her hands wide. 'Do you think it a great passion?'

'No,' Anna admitted. 'But deep, all

the same. A secure and contented thing.'

'Exactly. Undemanding. It takes nothing of her. Besides, not for many years did she marry — not until she was already *assoluta*.'

'And you've chosen that way, too. It seems hard, Nina.'

'Sometimes. But I love the dance.' She smiled, an impish and infectious smile, and Anna was almost persuaded that such a way of life could be right.

James brought in the tea then, complaining of the time the kettle took to boil and the fact that the sugar was in a tin marked 'Rice'.

'But you know I never keep anything in the right place,' Anna said on a faint note of warning. He looked at her in momentary incomprehension, and then understood.

'Oh, yes, of course — but sometimes a dull life is easier.' He glanced at Nina with a little, slightly shamefaced look, as though for the first time he, too, found deception uncomfortable.

When she had drunk a cup of very sweet tea — although the sugar was no longer necessary, she had begun to feel quite herself again — Anna took her two cassettes of film into the dark-room and started to develop them. Nina said that she must rest before the evening's performance, and went down into her own flat, insisting that before she went to bed Anna must call there to meet Sonya. James wandered aimlessly about, inspecting the decoration so far as it had gone, and eventually taking off his jacket, rolling up his sleeves and continuing the work, covering the unfinished walls of the hall at amazing speed. So an unexpectedly pleasant domestic evening evolved, James painting, Anna processing the films and cooking omelettes at a suitable moment, having dashed out to the off-licence at the corner of the street for a bottle of wine. Really, it was all very much as though she and James actually were engaged. She was coming almost to believe in it.

After supper she was able to make prints from the film. The negatives had looked good, and proved when enlarged to be so; some of them were more than good, they were breathtaking. Anna looked at the prints from the frames she had chosen to enlarge, and felt a kind of awe, to think that she had made these dramatic, stylish pictures, dancers seen in close-up and from angles that enhanced their curiously unreal beauty, making the casual eye pause and look again.

'Superb!' James breathed in delight and triumph. 'I *knew* you could! That group is magnificent — one can almost feel the texture of those tutus. For God's sake how did you judge the exposure time?'

'Inspired guesswork, or prayer, or something.'

'Fantastic! And this one of Baran — it actually seems to catch that feeling of suspension at the top of the leap! And his face — the effort, the exhilaration — oh, fabulous! You've caught the flying hair, and the spread of those fingers as though they're clutching at the air — '

'You think Lensky will like them?'

'I'm absolutely sure he will. I think we let him use what he wants of them, don't you?'

'If you think so. What would he use them for?'

'Oh, publicity — programmes, papers, *Dance and Dancers* and such magazines. Pretty good for you, you know — if you insist on an understanding that you're credited every time they're used.'

'I suppose so.' Anna felt once again utterly unbelieving. 'James, I seem to be about to be launched, and I'm not sure that I'm yet seaworthy.'

'Unsinkable, my dear — I guarantee it.' And such was his confidence that it carried her, and she could almost believe him.

He accompanied her to the theatre a little later, to leave a sheaf of prints with the doorman for Lensky. It was nine o'clock; the performance was still in progress.

'You want him, Miss?' the doorman inquired.

'No,' said Anna, feeling too tired for another interview with Lensky that night. 'Just see that he gets them, please. I'll see him tomorrow.'

James went on home after that, and Anna returned to her own flat and tumbled wearily on to the sofa, intending to wait until she heard Nina return, and then to go down. Such was her weariness that she fell at once into a black, timeless sleep, waking at last very much later, wondering if she had dreamed it, or if the doorbell of her flat had just rung.

6

It was the front door bell. It shrilled again, unnaturally loud in the silent flat. Anna groggily sat up, steadying her reeling head between her hands and wondering who it could be. Her wrist-watch said five minutes to midnight. Nina, perhaps, she thought; Nina, wondering why she had not been downstairs to meet Sonya.

But it was not Nina. A totally unknown man stood outside her door; he wore a peaked cap and close-fitting jacket, and held out to her an envelope, starkly addressed to Anna March.

'If you please, Miss, I'm to wait.'

'Oh.' Blankly, Anna took the envelope from him and tore it open, feeling that so many extraordinary things had happened to her recently that one more ought not to surprise her; besides, she was still half-asleep.

'I would like to speak with you,' the message said in a spiky, rapid and imperious hand. 'My car is waiting, and my man will bring you. Baran.'

For a moment she could not take it in. Then incomprehension gave way to astonishment, then fury. The impudence! — to think that she would drop everything and come at his bidding, like a slave — and at this time of night, without warning, without any guarantee of safe return —

'You'll be quite all right, Miss,' the manservant said impassively, as though he read her thoughts. Anna looked at him more closely. He was at least English, and looked reassuringly normal, a middle-aged man with a homely sort of face and faintly watery blue eyes. She felt that she had seen him somewhere before.

'You've seen me at the theatre,' he said, again with uncanny accuracy. 'I'm his dresser, too.'

Anna felt somewhat reassured.

'But it's midnight,' she pointed out. 'I

don't normally go out visiting just at midnight.'

'He's not, if you'll forgive the presumption, a normal sort of gentleman, is he, Miss? And a night bird. The owl's got nothing on him. Midnight to him is much like mid-day to you or me.'

'Well — ' Anna looked helplessly at the note. She felt all in confusion, with a restless excitement — maybe only curiosity — stirring in her blood; she was suddenly not at all tired. Here might be a chance to make a more amicable approach to Baran — she dared not let imagination run to anything more, though the sweet ache spreading through all her veins insisted on a more reckless hope. Perhaps, she told herself, he had seen the prints she had left for Lensky this evening — perhaps he wanted to apologise . . .

'I'll come,' she said. 'But — will you come in and wait a moment?'

'Thank you, Miss.' The man stepped into the hall. Anna indicated the chair, pointed out the patches of wet paint to be avoided, and then went into her bedroom. She had begun to tremble, gripped by a sense of daring, of adventure. He had sent for her; she would see him in his home, and that was at least to learn more about the enigma than most people ever knew. She was not, after all, a child — not any longer the shy and self-contained Anna March of Midhampton. She was quite capable of making Alexei Baran one way or another come to terms with her. He was not God, and she would not let him play at being so.

She resisted the urge to change out of her jeans and shirt. She would not give him the satisfaction of thinking that she had dressed especially for his benefit. Quickly she brushed her long hair, freshened her face, put on a suede jacket, and returned to the waiting manservant.

'Where does he live?' she asked.

'Top of a block in Brompton,' the man rather unexpectedly said. 'Had to be somewhere high up. Hates being in a crowd, he does.'

'There has to be a word for it,' murmured Anna dryly, thinking how typical it was of Baran to want to be both exalted and unique.

She scribbled a quick note for Nina, apologising for not having looked in and explaining that she had been summoned by Monseigneur. There were no lights and no sounds of wakefulness in the Rodzinska flat when she put the note through the door. Nina was evidently following the Lensky regimen of early nights. She followed the manservant — whose name she established as the reassuringly ordinary Smith — down the rest of the stairs to where a staggeringly impressive Rolls waited by the kerb, taking up almost half the street. Sinking into the luxurious ivory leather padded depths of the back, she was struck by a pang of regret that it wasn't daylight and there was no one to see her; she would rather have liked to have been seen getting into such a car. It seemed a natural sequel to walking with her recent degree of nonchalance in and out of stage doors, as though she quite belonged to that world. One couldn't fall much deeper into fantasy than this.

The car slid away so smoothly that she was unable to decide at just what point its movement began. The streets of the West End were still quite busy, a great many people wandering along the pavements, gazing into lighted windows, or emerging in glittering, animated crowds from clubs and restaurants. There were all-night cinema shows getting under way, all-night coffee bars and amusement arcades still doing trade. Neon lights cast an unreal garishness over figures, faces, the façades of buildings, so that Anna's sense of dreaming increased; it all looked like a very good film set, the background for a modern ballet, with the crowds milling about it to set the scene in to which the principal dancers would presently come.

South of Hyde Park the crowds

thinned, and along Knightsbridge there were few people. The Rolls turned off into side streets that Anna had never explored. Here there was a curious mixture of buildings, tall Victorian mansions standing close up against modern blocks of flats which gave way to garden squares, and at the end of one cul-de-sac an unexpected church. The Rolls at last drew in to the court in front of one of the new blocks, an expensive-looking, glassy monolith, with red carpet and flowers in the foyer and an awning over the steps up to the plate-glass doors. Smith ushered Anna before him, deferential, the perfect manservant. He took her across the foyer to the gilded doors of the lift, and pressed the button; the doors slid discreetly, smoothly open, and they stepped in. Even the lift was carpeted, and lined with pale rose watered silk. Anna, hollow and apprehensive, wished that there were a mirror, and that she had after all changed into something more prepossessing than her jeans and soft cotton shirt; more fervently still she wished that she had declined the invitation and stayed at home. But it had not been an invitation. It had been a command, and it had come from Alexei Baran; and by Baran she was hypnotised, her impulse was all instinctively towards him. She wanted to know what went on in his mind, what kind of a man he really was — and she wanted him to notice her. In that, perhaps, she was no different from many another star-struck adolescent, except that for her, now, opportunity presented itself. She was terrified by the realisation of what might depend on it, being so far from clear in her own mind as to what she really wanted.

The lift rose smoothly, noiselessly to the very top. They walked out of it into a lobby that was softly lit and silent underfoot. The door facing them had on it a single name engraved on a metal plate: Baran.

Anna hoped that Smith could not feel her trembling as he ushered her in, a hand lightly under her elbow. In the hall inside, which was but for a thick blue carpet entirely bare, he took her coat and then indicated a closed door at the far end, facing them.

'Knock and go in,' he said.

For a moment terror seemed about to swallow her alive. Then she remembered the determination with which she had set out, not to be afraid of him, not to let him browbeat her. She advanced on the door and rapped sharply, and when a voice commanded 'Come!' she opened the door and went boldly into the room.

It was astonishment that stopped her just beyond the threshold. There had been no particular expectation in her mind of what she would see, but whatever she might have pictured as Baran's chosen environment, it would not have been this.

She saw a vast, long room almost entirely bare of furniture. There was a shiny, smooth board floor, stretching it seemed into infinity. Thrown down as if at random there was a mattress covered in striped ticking and surrounded by cushions and tumbled blankets; there were suitcases standing about as they had been dumped down, some of them spilling rummaged clothes out on to the floor. There were books along one wall, standing on shelves of unpainted planks supported by building bricks. The whole of the opposite wall was window, uncurtained and showing beyond it limitless depths of purple night sky on which as if in a mirror the room was reflected, herself included, standing witlessly just inside the door and staring.

By the window Baran stood, watching her reflection, his back to the room. He was all in black, his feet bare. He did not turn for a moment or two, but continued to watch her image on the glass.

'I hardly thought you would come,' he said. His voice had a soft, curiously hypnotic quality. Anna felt that she ought to make some spirited, crushing reply, but could not find within herself the necessary impetus; she was thrown completely off her guard by the strangeness of the room, and by her own sense of embarking upon a dream.

'Why not?' she asked him.

'You are English — and a well brought up young woman.'

'I came because I wanted to. Curiosity, probably.' She came forward into the room now, and at last he turned to look at her. Without saying anything more he approached her, his bare feet silent on the board floor; she stood, and he circled her, examining her with bright, curious eyes as though she were some entirely unfamiliar object. He reached out to lift a strand of her thick, dark hair, and let it fall, watching it as it tumbled on to her shoulder. Anna stood as though she were carved out of marble; indeed, her flesh felt so, cold with excitement and fear, though her heart somewhere far inside her pounded and pounded its insistence on her power to move should

145

she need to do so.

'Why do you marry James Farmer?' he then astonishingly asked, his burning grey eyes searching her face as though he might read there some unsuspected reason.

'Why — why do you ask?' she stammered, not knowing what to say.

'Because I want to know. It seems to me extraordinary.'

'Why?'

'He is a very ordinary man. You are not at all ordinary. I can't imagine that you will be happy.'

'He's a wonderful person!' declared Anna, stung to defend her pseudo-fiancé. 'He's understanding and kind, thoughtful, clever — '

'But without great passion. That you will find a disappointment.'

'Oh!' She could not have felt more outraged had James indeed been her chosen husband. 'It really isn't any of your business — '

'But I find it fascinating. Come.' He indicated the pile of multi-coloured cushions spilling over from the mattress on the floor. 'You don't mind sitting on these? I dislike conventional furniture.'

Wordless, Anna curled herself down on to the cushions. They were surprisingly comfortable — more so than the granule bags in her own flat. Suddenly it occurred to her that a stranger going into her sitting-room would find it just as odd as this room of Baran's.

'I don't have much furniture, either,' she said, and then, having said something personal and unpremeditated, felt shy. Baran, sinking with one smooth, lithe movement on to the striped mattress, looked uncertainly at her, a flicker of some emotion — surprise, perhaps — briefly lighting his eyes.

'To me it means prison,' he said. 'It ties one down to a place, and I cannot be still in one place for long.'

'With me, it's just that I haven't yet got round to acquiring it,' she confessed. 'Though, to tell the truth, I quite like being without — I mean, one doesn't miss it.'

147

'One can get through life with amazingly little.'

'For a dancer I'd have imagined that was necessary. Because of travelling, I mean — and — perhaps for emotional freedom, too.' She said it with a certain caution, not wanting to sound as though she had swallowed the Lensky doctrine on the subject quite wholesale. Baran, lounging with a beautiful, relaxed indolence on the mattress beside her, regarded her with narrowed and cynical eyes.

'So you have been listening to *le Maître*, like a good little girl.'

'To one of the dancers, actually. But don't you agree with Lensky's ideas?'

'I don't know.' He looked suddenly moody and unhappy; she was vividly reminded of her photographs of him on the theatre roof. As if without his volition, his eyes turned to the one picture that the room possessed, a large black-and-white photograph above the bookshelves, of Blaise as Odette in *Swan Lake*. 'It may be necessary to keep one's life empty — there is little room for much besides the dance. But one becomes empty inside, one becomes barren — that can't be good.'

'But you have such privileges — you travel the world, you are wealthy and famous — '

'I go from airport to hotel room, to theatre dressing-room, I see little but anonymous crowds who are grasping and noisy — and, to be frank, who frequently smell. I am followed by the Press, who invent stories when they can find nothing else to write about. And the cameras are always there, boring little holes into my head.' He shrugged, as though he had long gone beyond the stage of resentment or anger, and had come to a despairing kind of acceptance. 'What one fears most, I think, is to give in to what they demand, to make some kind of a show for them, to cease to be oneself and become the image instead. Sometimes the temptation to do that frightens me.'

Anna's heart felt bleached with

sudden understanding of what that constant fear might be like, a kind of terror of losing one's identity for ever, of coming to believe what was written about oneself in the papers until one existed only at that remove and ceased to be real at all. It was a nightmare such as she hoped never to dream.

'But you are alive when you dance,' she said, trying to find reassurance for herself as much as for him. 'That, surely, is what you really are. That must give you a sort of absolute certainly to hold on to.'

'So I tell myself. But then, to dance is to become something not myself entirely. One plays a role on the stage. And I am not allowed just to dance — I am expected to be a sideshow as well.'

'You began in the West so dramatically, running away from the Russian company you were with in London and asking for asylum here. It made you at once a household name. And then, you do photograph so beautifully.' She couldn't keep a note of real feeling from her voice. He smiled, a brief, wintry gleam of amusement.

'You are, then, as passionate for your vocation as I am for mine.'

'I love pictures,' she said simply. 'And I love faces that make good pictures. I can't help it.'

'Does it not haunt your dreams, that you steal a little of someone with every picture that you take of him?'

'I don't think of it that way. I don't feel that I rob anyone.'

'But you do — of a look, a moment — an expression of themselves, something that should be only theirs — '

'Just looking at them does that, then.'

'No — because a look lasts only so long as the moment, but you make permanent something never intended to be so, you make of it an object for others to look at — ' He shook his head as though he despaired of being able to explain. 'You would make of my soul a graven image,' he said. 'And there are those foolish enough to worship it.'

She could think of no adequate reply.

'I am told that I must apologise to you,' he said at last. 'So, I apologise.' For just one moment the fine nostrils flared, as though even half in jest it was too much for him to ask forgiveness of anyone. Anna faintly smiled.

'That's why you sent for me?'

'No.'

'Then why?'

'I was curious. Also bored.' He turned his head as the door just then opened and Smith entered, dressed now in a white jacket rather like a waiter and propelling an impressively bottle-laden trolley.

'You will drink?' asked Baran, rising to his feet in another smooth and effortless movement — like a python, she thought suddenly; she had been trying to compare his grace of movement with that of a cat, a panther, but python was the word that reared up and lodged itself in her mind.

'Thank you.' She smiled at Smith, who gravely retreated, the discreet and perfect manservant. 'I like gin and tonic, but mostly tonic.'

'How proper.'

'I have to be. I'm not very much used to drinking.'

'No? But you look' — he shrugged — 'worldly. No — that's not right. But you have a certain absolute confidence — '

'It's very recent — and very thin.'

'Tell me.' He handed her a glass in which, after a cautious sip, she found the gin and tonic surprisingly to be in the proportions she had asked for; he himself sat again on the mattress, a glass of brandy in his hand. Anna took another sip of her drink, and then found it unexpectedly easy to begin on an account of herself, her uneventful past in Midhampton and the present in Bloom Street. He listened with intense concentration, as if it were some story he had to learn at first hearing, and there was something in his expression that seemed to speak of a kind of incredulity, as though such a place as Midhampton were entirely outside any experience of his — as indeed it must be, Anna thought. He could have no experience whatsoever of anywhere remotely like Midhampton.

'And this James Farmer?' he asked at once when she had done. 'You say nothing about him.'

'Oh — I met him when I took over his flat,' she hastily amended, having entirely forgotten her supposed engagement.

'And were so soon betrothed? That was impulsive.' His tone was undisguisedly sceptical.

'One knows at once,' she said defensively.

'Ah — love at first sight! How touching — and how misleading!'

'Haven't you ever been in love?' she dared. For a moment then she was afraid; his eyes flashed danger, the violence in him seemed visibly to coil ready for unleashing. But somehow the moment passed without any open outburst of anger.

'I do not care to put romantic labels

on what I have experienced,' he said. 'I am a realist. I know that I will never love a woman as much as I love the dance, and women are not content to come second in a man's life. So — ' He shrugged. Anna tried to think clearly. It was difficult, because she had to maintain the pretence of love for James when all her sensations and her thoughts were thrown into a turmoil by Baran himself. There were moments when she could almost convince herself of the reality of the person she must seem to him to be, confident, experienced, able to cope — and then the confidence would crumble, the knowledge engulf her that she was nobody at all in Baran's world, that she had never been actually in love with anyone attainable. All her affairs of the heart had been strictly one-sided, directed towards objects of impossible and starry grandeur. She could recognise her own fear of ever trusting any man close enough to be able to hurt her, because she remembered how deeply and for how many years her mother had suffered. But she could not tell Baran these things; nor could she tell him how confused she was now that one of the distant stars had come close enough for his brilliance to burn and blind her. She sat in the big, strange, bare room and looked at Alexei Baran, looked at him with concentration, as though she saw him now for the first time and must learn every feature. She knew from countless photographs the high Slav cheekbones, the wide brow, the finely chiselled moulding of nose and mouth, the full lips where sensuality and a streak of cruelty seemed to show. Pictures could not reproduce the strange, burning grey of his eyes, neither did photographs give much impression of the mobility of the features or of the swift, unexpected sweetness of his smile. He was known and yet unknown. His image had always attracted her, and unthinkingly she had built up round it a character, filling out details from her imagination. What she must do now was to banish that imaginary person from her mind so that she might see instead the real, complex and difficult man. It urgently mattered to her that she should do this. She felt in some way profoundly involved; it was as if in response to him parts of her being came alive for the first time, so that she was filled with strange new sensations, visions, understanding. She glimpsed a world beyond herself into which she wanted to go, and yet scarcely dared, being uncertain of her safety there.

'Sometimes, I think, we are afraid of involvement so much that we look for excuses not to get involved,' she said now, slowly.

'You think one should not take the precaution of avoiding pain?'

'I don't know. I begin to wonder if pain isn't perhaps — one of the things by which we know we are alive.'

'Oh, I am alive!' Abruptly he sprang to his feet as though violent movement released some unbearable tension. He paced barefoot and silent to the great wall of windows. 'Come,' he commanded her. 'Look.'

She got up and joined him, and gasped in involuntary astonishment and delight. All across the world, it seemed, as far as the horizon, a great jewelled carpet of lights was spread. She had not known that a city could be so beautiful. She could see the line of the river, a curling band of darkness edged with glittering beads.

'That is humanity,' Baran said. 'I watch it, and I am amazed.'

'But don't you belong?'

'I live as far above as I can get. There are too many things about being human that I don't like.' He looked at his wrist-watch. 'I cannot sleep tonight. Will you walk with me?'

'Walk?' Because it was so unexpected, stupidly she could make no sense of it.

'Sometimes I walk through London at night. It has then a kind of raddled beauty — and peace. Have you ever seen the sun come up in a great city? London is then like a whore dreaming of her girlhood. You should see it.'

'Well — yes, I'll walk, then,' said Anna, feeling beyond astonishment. 'But how do you find the energy to dance when you — ?'

'Oh, I need little sleep — and I take a cat-nap here and there. It is good to anger Lensky — I count it one of my pleasures.'

'You don't agree with all of his theories?'

'One cannot be Diaghilev any more,' he said simply.

He called Smith, who brought Anna her coat and Baran a short fur jacket and black leather boots, fur-lined and high like a Cossack's. Thus attired they went down in the lift and out into the by now chilly night air, and began their walk.

It was a night that afterwards Anna could remember only in fragments, each vivid memory separately attached to a place or to a subject of conversation, or to some sudden new discovery about him. They walked sometimes a little apart, sometimes arm in arm like close friends or lovers; they wandered along streets, alleys, parks, through closed and silent markets. Several times they came upon the river, standing each time for a little while looking out over the black, oily, shiny water as though there were some hidden secret to be discovered there. Conversation was spasmodic, with an ebb and flow of its own, unforced and natural; Anna came very soon to feel as though this were all part of some continuing dialogue from her own inner life, from her past. Sometimes it was as though each secretly knew what the other thought, but asked for the pleasure or the comfort of hearing it spoken in words. At other moments Anna's sense of new discovery was breathtaking, and the exploring of another, unknown mind seemed the most exciting, compulsive thing she had ever done. She hesitated to speak of ballet because it was his work, his life, and she in comparison knew very little, but he drew comment out of her and listened with attention to what she had to say. About pictures they came eventually to some degree of cautious agreement. The rest of their conversation was on generalities or arose from things they encountered on their walk. Amazingly Anna did not feel at all tired. She felt, on the contrary, elated and exalted, clearer in mind and vision than she had ever been in her life. It would have seemed right for this night, this walking and talking to have gone on for ever. But it could not. The sky grew pale, the lights dimmed; the sun at last came up, and they were almost at Bloom Street. Everywhere was asleep, the streets lay silent and empty in the innocent new light.

In the shadow of the doorway of Anna's house they stopped. Now at last she felt tired; her legs ached and her face was stiff from fatigue. Nevertheless she felt still sheltered by his arms, warm and at peace with him as though she belonged as close to him as this.

'How will you get home?' she asked him.

'A taxi. There are always taxis by now.' He put a hand under her chin, tilting her face so that he could examine it, doing so with a curious detachment, clinically, like a doctor looking for significant signs. 'So — thank you, Anna, for walking with me.'

'I — never enjoyed anything so much,' she said, unable to pretend.

'You do not love James.' It was a statement. Because she could not convincingly contradict it she remained silent. He looked intently at her for a moment longer. Then, gently, almost experimentally, he kissed her.

The strength, the violence of her own response amazed and frightened Anna. She clung to him; the kiss became more ardent and intense than any she had ever thought to give or to receive. Helpless and on fire, she trembled in his arms, wanting it never to end, wanting somehow to find oblivion, the answer, the end this way. It was he who at last drew away, looking down at her a moment more with fierce grey eyes that blazed and blinded her. Gently, then, he pushed her through the open doorway into the house, and turned and was gone on rapid feet into the growing light of the morning, without a further word.

7

Anna would not have thought it possible that she should sleep, so chaotically seething were all her thoughts and emotions. Nevertheless, falling again fully dressed on to her bed, she was asleep before there was time to begin on the self-searching that threatened her. But it was not this time a deep sleep, and it was troubled not by dreams but by sensations, by wild feelings of happiness, of elation, of doubt and dread and unbelief. She seemed in the misty depths of sleeping to be walking through whirling clouds and stars in a great lofty vault of night, and he — there was no face, no definite identity to the man beside her, but she knew him for the man she loved. It was not an easy or a tranquil love, but a consuming passion against which she was powerless to move; she was tied to him by a fate not of her own making, by a design formed out of the elements of the universe in the very birth of time.

She awoke in broad daylight, with a pigeon cooing at her from the window-ledge. Her head ached and her throat burned. She could not for a moment remember what had happened in the night.

When memory came back she struggled to sit up on the bed, feeling hot colour flood her face, scalding all over her. Could it really have happened like that? She had walked and talked with him all through the dark hours, sharing his curious, lonely vigil, and there had seemed to be a closeness and understanding between them much deeper than any she had ever before experienced with any man. And then, in that one spell-bound moment of the dawn, he had kissed her.

She had betrayed herself. The great need, the hunger stored deep down inside her, had been released by that kiss; she had responded with a desperate violence that must have shocked him. For surely his kiss had been a gentle, cool and friendly thing, a gesture as it were sealing the new friendship between them. It hadn't been meant as anything more. But she had seized upon it like a — like a sex-starved virgin avid for experience, hungry for love. And now all hope of friendship was destroyed. Their growing closeness had been sundered for ever by the recklessness of her response to that one kiss.

She wanted to weep, but tears would not come; it was as though she were quite dry inside. She got up from the bed, feeling cold and sick and crumpled. Her hair was a tangled mess, her shirt limp and clinging. Miserably she trailed through to the kitchen, and had just put the kettle on when the doorbell rang.

It was Nina, effervescent with curiosity.

'Come in,' Anna said dully. 'I'm just making coffee.'

'My dear!' Nina was in the kitchen with a skip and a hop, light and crisp as a blown leaf, her eyes glowing with delight. 'You were *really* summoned by Monseigneur? I had gone to bed — I found your note just now. Tell me!' She settled at the table, all agog. Anna tried to stop her own head from banging like a steam engine, begging Nina to wait until she had swallowed some coffee and aspirins.

'Oho! The hangover! *Très intéressant*. Also,' Nina admitted with some sympathy, 'very uncomfortable.'

'I didn't get home till daylight. It's lack of sleep more than a hangover.'

'You spent the *whole* night with him? La la! But the prestige!'

'Not merited, I assure you.' Sitting opposite her at the little kitchen table, and fortified by strong coffee, Anna began to feel slightly better. An atmosphere of unreality pervaded the memory of the night's events — yet, when she dared to think of that kiss, it was as though she felt his lips on hers again with all their strange, unnerving sweetness. That was still entirely real.

'But what happened? What did he want?' Nina persisted.

'He was curious. Lensky showed him the prints of the film I exposed yesterday, and, being fair-minded, he had to admit that they were good. Lensky and Marcia had been on at him to apologise to me, so he sent Smith for me — just at midnight.'

'Cinderella in reverse — you went to the ball at midnight!'

'It was very strange. His flat, Nina — at the top of a tower, like an eagle's nest, and just about as cosy. No furniture. Just a picture of Blaise as Odette, and a mattress on the floor. So lonely! It's right what everyone says — he is lonely and unhappy. When he can't sleep he walks about London all night. That's what we did — we walked until it was daylight.'

'But how very interesting, that he should want your company. He so seldom wants anyone at all. Oh, there are rumours, you know, about some-times wild parties, expensive women

— but never close friends.'

Anna closed her eyes and shook her head. She did not understand, either, why he should have wanted her company once he had made the obligatory apology. At the time there had been a kind of inevitability about it; they had seemed quite simply to become close — to be in some mysterious way tied by delicate, invisible threads which it would have been churlish to have broken. But now, in the light of morning and of common sense, it seemed all inexplicable and strange.

She could not tell Nina about the kiss. It mattered too much; she burned with shame when she thought of it; and burned, too, with a fierce remembered ecstasy which shame could not subdue.

'What will James say?' wondered Nina, and brought down a cold douche of reality upon Anna's reflections. James. She had forgotten James.

'I'm sure he won't at all mind,' she said with more truth than Nina could know. Even Nina, surely, could not think James a particularly possessive or jealous fiancé, now that she knew him and had seen him together with Anna. 'He'll regard it as all good for the book, I should think.'

'He is very sensible,' Nina agreed. 'But, my dear, consider — you are unique! The first photographer in history to have conquered the ferocious Alexei Baran. You are *made*!' Nina's eyes shone with genuine delight; she clapped her hands in glee, infectious and irresistible. Anna could not in the face of this maintain her total despondency. There was, after all, a lighter side if one could only keep it in view. To him a kiss was — well, very little. He was a worldly sophisticate, and to kiss a pretty girl on the doorstep must be a matter of routine, no more than a handshake. He lived in the world of the theatre, where everyone kissed everyone. Doubtless her response had disconcerted him, but he was unlikely to make much of it, beyond perhaps feeling a certain amusement at such confirmation of a naïvetée to which, after all, she had freely confessed. He might feel also that it proved the unsuitability of her match with James. But that really wasn't his business.

She must try to see it in those terms, Anna told herself, and by this mechanism of self-defence came almost to believe that the episode had meant nothing.

It wasn't until she entered the theatre with Nina some time later, intending to photograph the morning's class, that she discovered her inability to maintain that belief. She stepped through the stage door, and at once her heart began to pound, her limbs to tremble; her hands became clammy and unsteady. She wanted to turn and run from the inevitability of meeting him. But she could not run away; she was bound by her agreement with James, if nothing else, and there was pride, too. Pride helped a great deal. Why should she be afraid? He, after all, had as much to be ashamed of — he had taken advantage of her inexperience. And he knew that she was engaged to another man.

She went into the salon in a state of rigid calm. Lensky was there with the ballet mistress. He seized her hands in his, beaming down at her through the thickness of his black beard, his autocratic features as near to expressing approval as they could come.

'It is a splendid talent!' he declared. 'Madame, this little girl has an eye which sees as as we would like always to be seen. She understands the ballet.'

Madame sharply nodded her head, the wrinkles of her face arranging themselves into a smile.

'Then it is good,' she said. '*Bien*. You photograph today?'

'I want to. Yesterday I watched, to see what could be done. There's more material, really, than on stage — '

'The class is the heart of the ballet,' declared Madame, with the air of one pronouncing a great truth.

'So,' Lensky asked Anna, 'you have already replaced the camera?'

172

'Not yet. This is my second camera.' She smiled at his expression. 'It's useful to have more than one, for running black and white film at the same time as colour, for instance, or to save changing lenses when you're working at speed.'

'I am glad, then, that there was no delay in your work. But you must get a new camera, all the same. Get one that is really worthy of what you are able to do with it, Miss March.'

'Thank you.' She felt warmed by his evident sincerity, and was at the same time incredulous to think that he, who could command the work of the best photographers to be had, should be so much taken with hers.

She went to her corner by the piano, smiling at the pianist, who was a young man but looked somehow aged as though he found his work tedious. In her preoccupation with the camera bag, putting lenses ready, checking film, readying the light, she was able to subdue her apprehensive longing to

173

watch the door until he should come in, and kept her back to the class, turning only once when the pianist made a little, terse clicking noise with his tongue and exclaimed 'Kirilova!' as though the name disgusted him. Anna saw that a woman had come in whose face she did not know, a lovely, delicately made blonde creature in a white leotard and immaculate tights which clung to long, long legs displaying hardly any of the muscle which Anna had come to accept as inevitable in a dancer. Kirilova. The name was distantly familiar. She danced, surely, mainly on the Continent with one of the German companies. Of course — she was here to dance *Giselle* and *Swan Lake*; her name was on the advance list over which Anna had pored, oh, it seemed a lifetime ago. She was to partner Baran. It was their first time of dancing together at the Imperial.

A lovely face, Anna thought, ignoring the unreasonable stab of jealousy that pierced her, firmly continuing to arrange her photographic equipment. And said to be a rising star; not yet the undisputed successor to Blaise, but . . .

Madame clapped her hands; the pianist's fingers hung poised.

'*Allons, mes enfants! Un, deux, trois* — '

Anna turned to survey the class.

He was there, in the place he had occupied yesterday, Blaise behind him and Kirilova in front. Anna looked once at him, and was shaken and devastated by the most intense and uncontrollable emotion. It was as though her heart for the first time achieved sensation, and felt unbearable pain; it was like death, or birth. He was there, only so short a distance from her and yet unreachable; she loved him and it hurt quite desperately.

With shaking hands, clumsily, she tried to adjust the camera, wildly pointing it anywhere but at him, biting her lips so that she would not cry out, savagely blinking back sudden hot tears which threatened to overflow. She was trembling so much that to take a clear picture was impossible. Thank God no one was looking at her — they had all that rapt, concentrated, inward look, all their attention upon the movement of their own bodies. Even he seemed unaware of her, though she felt that the intensity of her agitation must surely reach him through the air.

Gradually she became calmer. It wasn't, after all, a new idea, that she loved him. She had known herself interested, attracted; she had even briefly, for a moment, admitted to love. But the word had not then meant what it meant now. She could not then have imagined this great wild, sweet aching through all her being, nor her sense of utter helplessness in its grip. Nor, then, had she known anything of the tenderness that filled her heart now as she looked at him once more, safe behind the camera. She knew so much about him now, about the strange thoughts inside that proud, beautiful and yet vulnerable head. She knew that he was lonely, imaginative and complex, that he was afraid to love, that he felt apart from humanity and did not relish his isolation. She knew that he could be kind, gay, arrogant, perceptive, cruel. She suspected a great capacity for love in him — and desperately, more than anything in the world, she wanted to arouse that capacity and to make him love her.

Which was, of course, a child's dream and could not come true.

Gradually she became steadier, and at last was able to detach her thoughts from him enough to take pictures, seeking out and finding shots she had planned yesterday, comforting herself with the abstract beauty of strong, supple limbs, of pliant arms and long throats, the lovely shadows under jaw and brow. She used a telescopic lens to go really close in to arched feet, so that the scuff marks and the darns on the shoes showed, as did the curious deformity of feet made to do things for which human feet were not designed. She had noticed his feet last night, bare upon the board floor; they were the only thing about him that was not beautiful, they were calloused and muscular and ugly.

Kirilova, on the contrary, contrived even to have elegant feet, long-boned and tapered as though they did not know the meaning of the word 'work'. And yet they went through the routine of the class with fine and spirited precision; their *battements* were executed with neat perfection, their points were diamond hard. The woman's face showed no effort; after half an hour of gruelling work, all rhythmic scuffing of shoes, beating, lifting, stretching, she was still fresh, only the faintest satin shine on her perfect skin betraying any warmth at all. The others had almost all begun to glisten with sweat; Anna took several shots of faces so close that the separate beads of perspiration could be seen, making a grainy texture that was in itself somehow exciting, emphasising the gruelling nature of what these dancers must go through to achieve their world-famous standard of perfection. She did not dare to look too often at Baran in case she should meet his eye; if at the end of the class he should speak to her, or she should find it impossible to avoid him, what was she to do? She could not imagine that any meeting between them could be other than embarrassed — on her side at least; he perhaps had splendid self-confidence enough to have laughed off the whole episode, or, even worse, to be indulgent towards her, amused at the response he had so easily aroused with one kiss. She did not know. After all, the closeness she had felt walking and talking with him through the dreaming city must have been an illusion; she did not know him. His face, when she dared briefly to train the camera lens on it, told her nothing save that he was utterly, single-mindedly involved in the work of the moment, no thought in his head save of how to achieve perfection.

This, she thought, was what the word 'dedication' meant; this was why no woman could hope for any great share in his life.

When the class came to an end, Anna, who had dreaded this moment, became suddenly busy with her camera, unnecessarily changing lenses, checking the number of spare films in her bag — waiting in an agony of nerves for him to be gone so that she could breathe again — and maybe, silently, weep. She sensed rather than saw Nina coming across the room to her, threading a way through the chattering crowd until suddenly something stopped her and she fell back into the general mêlée. Panic leapt — too late. Baran was before her, his hand under her chin forced her head up so that she must look at him.

Her eyes felt dazzled, blinded; she could not meet his gaze.

'Good morning,' he said at last, a very faint edge to his soft voice. 'You do not seem so well disposed towards me.

What have I done? Is it the righteous anger of an outraged little girl, after all?'

She shook her head and struggled to find words, but for very weakness none would come.

'You have perhaps seen James this morning?'

'No.'

'You fear to see him? You have a conscience, maybe? Or you have seen the truth of what I said, that you are not for him?' He waited for some response, and then, when none came, shrugged and impatiently turned away. 'And then, maybe I was mistaken in you. Maybe, after all, you suit him very well.'

It was on the tip of Anna's tongue to say 'no' once more. She turned her head aside, about to shake it in denial, and caught the gaze of Lensky's dark and gleaming eyes. He was watching their every movement; he had quite probably caught almost everything that had been said, and he looked danger-ous. Anna checked the denial, and remained dumb. Baran abruptly walked away from her, striding back to the *barre* where Kirilova was admiring in the mirror her perfect reflection.

'The principals remain to rehearse *Giselle*,' said Nina, coming quietly to Anna's side. 'One may wait and watch. Will you do so?'

Desperately Anna tried to collect herself. She suddenly felt that if she did not get away somewhere and weep, she would burst. She ought to stay to photograph Baran and Kirilova, but she could not bear to do so.

'I'll get my things together and go home,' she told Nina, her voice tight and insecure with the pressure of unshed tears. 'My head aches.'

'Shall I come? I don't *want* to stay.'

'Come with me.' She felt that Nina's sympathetic, worldly presence would be a comfort; she couldn't bear any longer to keep to herself what she felt. Hurriedly, with trembling hands, she tucked the camera equipment into the bag, checking that everything was there.

Already the piano had begun the Act One music, and in the middle of the cleared salon Kirilova and Baran took up their places for their first *pas de deux*, Giselle and her disguised lover. Against the mirrored walls round the room many of the class had stayed to watch. Anna felt horribly conspicuous as she and Nina made their way past this scattered audience to the door; she could feel the eyes of Lensky burning into her back, and was in sudden terror that he would at the last moment call her and prevent her escape. But he did not do so. She reached the door, Nina ahead of her, and plunged thankfully out into the cold air of the corridor. Even then, in all the agony of fear and embarrassment and misery that engulfed her, she was not so blind that she did not see Marcia Blaise standing just inside the salon doorway, watching as Baran and Kirilova embarked on their *pas de deux*, a look in her great dark eyes of limitless sadness.

It was the most fleeting of impressions; a moment later Anna could not quite believe in it. All the same, it had been extraordinarily vivid and it stuck in her mind to be examined and interpreted later.

Nina was swathed in a great blanket-like cloak; indeed, it was a blanket, Anna decided on closer examination.

'I must shower at once. Come into my flat? Sonya will be back a little later, but we must talk. You have things to say, *ma chère*. There must be no more pretending.'

'You bully me!' Anna complained, thankful all the same to be bullied. It was, perhaps, what she needed. She followed Nina up the stairs of the Bloom Street house to the second-floor flat, and sank gratefully into an armchair in the comfortable, untidy sitting-room while Nina disappeared into the bathroom. There was time to think now. What was she to do? How much could she safely tell Nina? Without consulting James she could scarcely betray the secret of the engagement, and yet how could she talk about what had transpired between Baran and herself without mentioning her supposed feelings for James? It was all the most foolishly tangled web — foolish because that aspect of her problems need never have become a problem at all, and now wretched and painful, since Baran must think her in some way under James Farmer's spell as she had not, given every chance, denied that she loved him. Believing that, how could any man so proud as Baran do other than entirely and ruthlessly put her out of his thoughts?

Nina came fresh and glowing from her shower, wrapped again in white towelling and soft as a kitten.

'Not, today, the coffee,' she said decidedly. 'I have a bottle for occasions such as this. Very good cognac, given to Sonya by an admirer who did not know that she hates the stuff.'

'You're trying to loosen my tongue.'

'No — only the terrible tight knots

inside which hurt you.' Nina produced the bottle from a cupboard, together with two glasses into which she poured a generous measure. Anna reflected as she took it that she had drunk more alcohol in the past few weeks than in the whole of her life before. Her Midhampton landlady would have been confirmed in her dark suspicions as to what befell innocent girls in London.

Combined with the sudden explosive fire of the cognac as she took her first sip, that thought triggered off a wild, hiccoughing fit of laughter which soon gave way to unstoppable tears. Nina nodded, and sat quietly by, having known that it must happen.

'So,' Nina said into the silence at last, when Anna had sobbed herself quite empty of tears. 'You see now, perhaps, the wisdom of what Lensky demands of us, that we avoid this terrible insanity called love.'

'But I didn't know it was happening until it had happened!' Anna snuffled miserably into her sodden handkerchief. 'What am I to do, Nina?'

'About whom? About Baran, or James?'

'Oh, about Baran. James — doesn't matter. No!' — as Nina made a little involuntary movement of indignation. 'You don't understand. I mean — he wouldn't be much hurt by it if he knew.'

'Ah. It is a cool passion, then? I had wondered.'

'It's — yes. Cool. It might not have come to marriage, anyway. But — that's not for anyone else to hear, Nina — please.'

'What do you think? Indeed, I say *nothing* of what we discuss now — nothing to anyone!' The girl was pink with serious indignation. Anna sought to soothe her, saying:

'No, I know, but it matters so much; I had to say it. Nina, if Lensky thought me capable of causing any disturbance, with Baran or anyone else, I'd not be allowed in the theatre again. And I do mind terribly much about these pictures.'

'I understand. All the same, you have caused — well, *quelque chose* with Monseigneur. I have never, *never* seen him make an approach to any woman as he did to you today. And then, last night — '

'He kissed me,' Anna blurted out, feeling better once she had actually said it. 'It didn't mean anything to him, I'm sure, but — to me it was — I don't know — it sent me for a few minutes quite insane. So he concludes that either I don't love James but won't admit it, or — oh, I don't know what he thinks! But he's angry with me, and it hurts.'

'But you idiot!' Nina exploded. 'Of course if he wants you himself he will be angry if you remain loyal to James! Why could you not — ?'

'Why should he want me? And if he did — which I can't, I just can't believe — in what way, and for how long? I haven't any way of knowing, Nina. I'm not in his league at all — I can't play sophisticated love games without getting hurt. I didn't want to love any man, ever — they're not worth it, they can't be trusted.'

'La! What a dismal tale! And James, did you not trust him?'

Anna tried to envisage James, to think of him clearly and without distortion. He did not seem at all real.

'Yes,' she said at last. 'Of all I feel about James, that's the most sure. He can be trusted, he's reliable. But that's nothing, is it, compared with being really in love?'

'I do not know,' said Nina slowly, a look of pre-occupuation on her face, as though she were testing the theory against some inner experience of her own. 'I think that one might fall very much in love with a man just because he was safe and faithful. But not so with Baran. If you love him, then you must be prepared to suffer. That is the law of passion.' She sighed. 'Listen, Anna. Today I watched him. I saw him many times look at you. Maybe he does not yet entirely love you — but I swear to you this: he is interested, he wants you. If you were to make up your mind to it, I think you could have him.' Her small, pointed, cat's face was serious, incongruously old and knowing; she nodded her head and looked wise, far beyond Anna in experience. 'And another thing I know,' she went on. 'The First Lady has also seen this. And she would a thousand times rather relinquish him — as she knows soon she must do — to you, than to Tatiana Kirilova. Had you not thought of that? You should; it is worth consideration.'

8

It was typical of James that he should wait until half past three in the afternoon before ringing her to ask how she had got on, whether Baran had apologised, and, rather as an after-thought, to say that he had tickets for the Festival Hall that evening.

'Martineau and the PSO,' he explained. 'I thought that since you'll sooner or later be photographing them you might as well have a look.'

It was a handle by which she could drag herself up out of the depths of apathy and self-pity into which she had sunk. Determined to make the most of it, she went shopping in the little that was left of the afternoon, and by the time that James called for her had, with Nina's help, achieved an appearance of considerable sang-froid in swathes of ivory cotton lace and elaborately looped and braided hair. But there were dark smudges under her eyes, and he noticed them.

'You mustn't let Baran get under your skin,' he insisted. 'There's nothing he can do unless you let him upset you.'

She wanted to laugh at the irony of it.

'It's not that, James. But the last few days have been hectic. Midhampton was never like this.'

'I keep forgetting how recently you emerged from the backwoods. All the same, tonight's a holiday. Let it be a real break.'

But even at the Festival Hall there were reminders of Baran. Sitting in the stalls, surrounded by people somehow different from those who normally occupied a similar place at the Imperial, Anna was trying to decide in precisely what the difference lay when she saw Max Silbermann sitting beside Helen Martineau, a little to their left and only two rows in front of them. James, who must have felt the little start she gave, followed her gaze.

'Oh, yes,' he said, 'Max is much more a straight music than a ballet man. Haven't you seen his photos of Martineau? Much more interesting and flattering than any Helen's ever done of her own husband — but then, her talent's very selective, she probably doesn't think Carlos worth the expenditure of film.'

'I don't like her much.'

'Understandable. But try to keep on the right side of her. She's influential. I'd like you to get some pictures of Szabo, the pianist, for instance, but you'll not get near him if she doesn't approve.'

'I don't like having to crawl. It makes me feel — ' She shrugged, unable to explain so that it didn't sound childish.

'If you want to succeed in a profession that lives off the appearance of celebrities, you must learn to minister to their vanity,' James told her, his voice and his glance very dry. 'At the same time you mustn't ever reflect back at them a true picture of the size of their own heads.'

'I'm beginning to learn that.'

'Baran came over with a handsome apology, though?'

'I'm not sure that the word 'sorry' was actually spoken, but the intention was there.' She could not tell him what had really happened. She felt as much trapped as if she were really engaged to him.

'We'll have a word with Max in the interval,' James said, catching the photographer's eye now as he looked round, and waving. 'Be interesting to hear what version he's had from Marcia.'

Anna felt helpless, as though whatever she did, wherever she went, events were weaving themselves steadily round her in soft, smothering threads so that escape was impossible. She knew now how the fly felt, embarked on a perilous crossing of a spider's web.

She tried to forget herself in the comforting familiarity of the Haydn symphony which began the programme. The music was sparkling and clear, as if it had been specially chosen as a contrast to her confusion of mind; Martineau and a much scaled-down orchestra gave it a witty, elegantly pointed performance. But she could not very much enjoy it.

The Rodriguez guitar concerto followed, with James Farnaby as soloist. For a little while then she did forget her problems in the contemplation of his strikingly beautiful head, wondering if she would have a chance to photograph him one day since he was so clearly worth it. There was a look about him, something rapt, absorbed and luminous, which reminded her of Baran. Dedication, perhaps, was the word that came closest to describing it. But, dedicated though he might be, Farnaby had a wife.

She refused to let herself think that way. Whatever happened she would never be Baran's wife. She did not belong to his world; she had merely strayed into it. Kirilova belonged. She was the kind of woman he might possibly one day marry. And Blaise

— Anna remembered the look in the First Lady's eyes as she had watched Baran prepare to partner the lovely Kirilova. A dark fire of pain had burned there; it had been the look of a woman who has dreamed long dreams, and knows that the day must now come and shrivel and fade her dream until nothing remains of it but memory. Marcia Blaise loved Baran. She was part of his life as Anna could never hope to be.

The interval came, and in the scramble to the bar Max Silbermann caught up with Anna and James.

'Coincidence that I should see you,' he said to Anna. 'I was with Mannings of the *Sunday News* this afternoon. He showed me your pictures of Baran which are going into this Sunday's magazine. Very fine!'

Anna's heart turned cold within her. Incredibly, she had managed to forget that in another day's time Baran would see those photographs. After that, had she any chance ever again of coming anywhere near him? It seemed unlikely.

'He hasn't seen them?' Max Silbermann asked, accurately reading her expression. 'I could not believe that he had done so and we had not heard the explosion. You are worried?'

'Yes,' she admitted miserably. James had gone ahead to the bar and was swallowed up in the crowd; Max drew Anna aside into a corner where they were a little sheltered from the worst of the crush.

'You must not let him frighten you into giving up,' Silbermann said earnestly. 'You have talent, and I like James' idea. Together you can produce something of real worth. New eyes are much needed in the ballet, to record the excellence of the work being done in London now.'

'But Baran is powerful — and he can make one feel — oh — '

'Did you send Mannings the prints?'

'No. Lensky did that.'

'Then Baran must spend his anger on Lensky, not on you.'

'But I took the wretched things.'

'You would not have published them, I think? No, that was Lensky — my dear, I *know* him! Also I know Baran, and I know that he has *au fond* a sense of fairness, an integrity. He must see that the pictures are beautiful. He will know that you took them because you are dedicated to the recording of beauty, and he understands dedication, having it himself. So he will forgive you.'

'Will he?' Doubtingly, Anna looked at him, troubled by knowledge which Silbermann did not possess. It was not quite so simple as it seemed. 'How can he not mind having his private unhappiness plastered all over a trendy Sunday supplement?' she demanded. 'I ought never to have taken the beastly photos. I feel as though I've — oh, betrayed a confidence, a friendship — ' Tears gathered hotly behind her eyes, and she found Silbermann's gently searching gaze difficult to bear. Presently he made a little, impatient tch-tch noise with his tongue and abruptly took her hand in his, patting it with fatherly concern.

'So! It is that way,' he said softly.

'I didn't say so.'

'Your eyes say everything. Don't trouble to deny what they tell me. I'm an old man and I have seen that look many times in my life. There is, my dear, a kind of pain that only love can inflict. Your eyes speak of it.' His ugly little face creased into a wry, clownish grin of self-deprecation. 'Come, now — what are we to do about it?'

'Nothing,' she said flatly. 'Nothing at all.' But she had a strong impulse to tell him everything. Angry at her weakness, she had to remind herself that this was Silbermann the photographer, husband to Marcia Blaise and friend to almost everyone who mattered in the arts. He wasn't some kindly, middle-aged uncle on to whose accommodating shoulder she could sob out her story, much as she longed to do so.

'Really,' she insisted, but more gently

199

now, 'I can't talk about something so nebulous as though it were accomplished fact. And if I could, it isn't really mine to tell. Anyway, it'll come right in time.'

'Human affairs seldom come right without help.'

'I'm capable of managing.'

'Rubbish! You are scarcely out of the egg. About such people as Baran you know nothing. He has *lived*, my dear. You have so far only existed.'

'How can you know that?'

'By looking at your face. It is untouched by experience.' A teasing note softened the words, and he was smiling; all the same, she knew that he was right.

'What can I do?' she asked him, the words coming out despite her feeling that she ought not to admit to anything. 'I've got so tangled up in a world that was only dreams until now. I don't know how much is in my imagination, how much real.'

'Are you dazzled by the glamour of

the theatre? By his fame?'

'Yes. No. I don't know. There are moments when I seem to see him just as a person — not as Baran.'

She stopped, and after a moment he said, 'You see, it matters to me. We love him, my wife and I.'

Swiftly Anna looked at him, to see how much the faint emphasis on the last words might mean. There was no teasing, no laughter in his eyes now, only a great and tolerant disillusionment.

'You both care?' she asked, carefully ambiguous.

'Marcia has a great gift for love. She is able also to allow herself to be loved, without demanding that it all be cut and dried and according to convention. She brought him into our lives, and he is part of us. But this cannot meet his needs for ever — there must come a parting. Do you understand?'

'I think so. But he — he seems naturally a solitary creature.'

'He is so much at odds with himself

that he must needs be also at odds with the world. His experience of love has not been happy. In many ways he is a selfish and wilful creature — after all, he has unique gifts and would be a fool not to know it. But that makes for loneliness, doesn't it? With whom can one share the experience of being unique? And so one grows selfish, and discontented.' Silbermann shrugged. 'But listen, my dear — I thought that all was settled between you and James?'

'Not absolutely.' Guiltily she fingered the still unfamiliar ring on her left hand. 'It's impossible to explain.'

'Do you love him?'

'No,' she admitted, since it was clearly impossible now to claim that she did so. 'I like and admire him, but — '

'Then you must not marry him! That would be wrong and foolish — oh, what a disaster it would be!'

'I don't see why. Marriages happen for less convincing reasons. It might be a great success.' But she could not believe her own protestations. Helplessly she shook her head, feeling defeated. 'Don't ask me any more, please.'

'I have been clumsy and interfering, but you must forgive me!'

Anna was saved from the need to reply by the sudden advent of James, bearing hard-won glasses from the bar and fluently cursing the slow service and the intractable nature of interval crowds. But all through the second half of the concert, against a background of Mahler, she concentrated her attention all inwards, trying to get clear in her mind what she must do. It wasn't possible to carry on the fiction of the engagement. Too much was at stake, now. Somehow, whatever the consequences, she had to make it clear to Baran that she was free. It might be of no interest to him, or his interest might be only the passing fancy of a man accustomed to take love as his due — and if he did at all care now, it was unlikely that he would still do so after the *Sunday News* had come out. All the same, regardless of pride, she must let him know that she was free and that she cared for his regard — cared, if she were truthful, more passionately than she had ever cared about anything else in the whole of her life.

She had no appetite for supper, and begged James to take her straight home after the concert. Briefly they went backstage, where Carlos Martineau greeted them like old friends and expressed his willingness for Anna to photograph a rehearsal at any time; Helen Martineau congratulated her — not without some acidity — on Max Silbermann's enthusiasm for the *Sunday News* pictures, and insisted that she must visit her own studio in the near future. In all the noisy crush of friends and fans it was not hard for Anna to plead convincingly that her head ached. James was troubled by it.

'You mustn't take it all so seriously,' he warned her in the taxi on the way home, in the most friendly and natural way drawing her close to him so that her head rested on his shoulder, where she felt like a child or a sister, but not at all like a woman in love.

'James, we have to stop pretending to be engaged,' she blurted out. 'It won't do — it's causing too much misunderstanding.'

'You find it difficult to pretend affection for me?' There was an attempt at teasing in his voice, but it wasn't entirely successful. Anna tried to read the expression in his eyes by the uneven lights of neon signs as the taxi passed through the late night streets. She wondered, suddenly appalled by the idea, whether he might not possibly have fallen in love with her himself. The notion was at once rejected; it was too absurd, James wasn't that sort of person. He was extremely sophisticated, worldly, and probably more in love with himself than he could be with any woman, whereas she was naïve, untutored in the ways of his world. But then, Nina had been quite willing to accept the notion of Baran's being attracted to her. Was it any less likely that James should find her desirable?

The seed of suspicion was sown, and she could no longer rest her head comfortably upon his shoulder.

'You know it's not that, James,' she said, sitting up. 'You're easy to like. But I don't want to be thought tied, by — by anyone to whom it might matter.'

'But that, my dear girl, was precisely the effect intended! Don't tell me you seriously want to start an affair with one of the company? Couldn't it wait until we've done all the work we want with them?'

'No,' she said, trembling with the effort of insisting on something so contrary to what they had planned. 'It's already caused — well, a misunderstanding.'

'What have you been up to in the last few days? You're a quick worker, I give you that!'

'I don't want to talk about it.'

'Very well.' He shrugged. He was not exactly angry, but she felt that he had become cool and rejecting; she hated the feeling of being shut out from him. Her head throbbed. She felt alone, insecure and thoroughly miserable. Suddenly there came into her mind a memory of that morning, so short a time and yet so long ago, when she had got out of bed feeling lonely, and had looked out of the window at the lovely autumn morning and had seen Baran. Her loneliness then had sprung from lack of involvement with the world. She was involved, now, more than she could ever have imagined that she would be, and yet still she was lonely, not able to feel that she belonged or that there was really a place for her among the people she had met. Would her life always be like that? It seemed as though she must be temperamentally unable to want what was readily available to her, but must always long for the far-off dream, the magical world just out of reach.

'You'd better consider yourself free, then,' James said to her after a long silence. 'But avoid, if you can, letting Lensky know. Try not to disrupt things.'

'You think me inept and trouble-some, don't you, James?'

'You don't seem to have grasped the need to merge with the background,' he said. 'You've fought with Baran, and you've given Lensky cause to wonder — '

'You've seen him?'

'He rang me this afternoon,' James said shortly. 'Just after I had rung you. He wanted to warn me that I must head you off Baran.'

'Oh, really!' She tried to sound scornful, but remembered Lensky's face as he had watched Baran approach her that morning in class. 'He can't think I'm capable of seducing Monseigneur — especially now that Kirilova has arrived.'

'You upset Kirilova, too. It was she who demanded of Lensky who you were and why you should have thrown Baran into such a dark depression. She has, of course, a vested interest.'

'It's all unspeakably petty and silly!' She was too near to tears to be able to say anything more, and yet beneath her anger and contempt there flared a tiny spark of hope. If her effect on Baran had really been so noticeable, there must, surely, be some truth in Nina's belief that he did a little care for her. And if that were so, then anything was possible, anything at all . . .

'Anyway,' James said with grim satisfaction, 'he goes abroad on Sunday night to dance in Vienna. You'll be able to get on with the job in peace then.'

'Abroad?' Anna's heart stumbled and grew cold. 'How long?'

'Oh, a week or so. You should have done by then with the Imperial.'

She said nothing more, for fear of saying too much. But that night in her uncurtained room, with the neon glow of the city eerily reflected from the ceiling, she could not sleep. Her limbs ached and her head burned; she felt like some desert hermit tormented by heat and thirst and by desire that could never be fulfilled, dreams to which she had no right. She loved Baran, but knew of no way to tell him so; she saw her love as a delusion, an infatuation, but could not rid herself of the fire and the pain of it. By the time that morning came she was in a fever of mind and body — a very real fever, since her whole body alternately blazed and shivered and she could hardly lift her head from her hot and crumpled pillow. She got to the kitchen for a drink, and then, too weak and too confused for anything else, got thankfully back into her bed and fitfully dozed or lay miserably awake until the doorbell at last roused her.

It was Nina, who took one horrified look at her feverish, watering eyes and white face, and marched her straight back to bed.

'You have at least the 'flu,' she pronounced. 'Poor, poor girl — you should have banged hard on the floor, or rung us. I shall get Dr Davies.'

'There's no need — '

'But there is. Anyway, he is madly in love with Sonya and is glad of the excuse to come to the house.'

Anna was too weak to protest. She had some confused awareness of being made more comfortable in bed by Nina, who was then joined by Sonya and eventually also by a capable young man who inspected her, pronounced a verdict of influenza and instructed them that they must give her aspirin and plenty to drink, and then vanished in the company of Sonya, leaving Nina to sit by her bed while she slipped in and out of troubled sleep. Darkness at some time came, and then she really slept, deeply and without dreams, to wake on the following day with a sense of comparative well-being.

She lay at first unmoving in her bed, looking at the reflection of pale sunshine on the ceiling, listening to distant, small sounds of movement somewhere in the house. The streets outside were very quiet — unnaturally so, considering that it was daytime. For a few moments she was puzzled, disorientated. Then she remembered that today was Sunday. Of course it was quiet, there was no business and very little life here on a Sunday. Once offices, shops and the market were closed it was a strangely deserted area.

Sunday! Awareness flashed through her like an electrical charge. Today her photographs of Baran would be spread across the pages of the *Sunday News Magazine*, and he would see how she had betrayed him. Tonight he would fly to Vienna, taking with him only revulsion and anger against her, believing that she was, after all, no more than the most hardened and cynical journalist to whom he was just another story. Anna was filled with the most painful agitation. She could not let it end so; she had to see him, to try to explain — at least to let him know that she had had nothing to do with the publication of the pictures.

'Nina!' she called hoarsely, struggling to sit on the edge of the bed, her head like a great ball stuffed with warm hay, her limbs aching as though they were bruised. Nina came hurrying in from the kitchen.

'*Tiens!* You must not get up yet, you will make yourself very bad! There, now, lie down and I will get you a drink.'

'Nina, I have to see him! Has the paper come? I must see him!'

'Here, here — ' Thinking that she meant only the photographs, Nina thrust into her trembling hands the magazine supplement which had been lying on a chair at the foot of the bed. 'They are very good — everyone says that your reputation is made. But you mustn't get excited — '

'Oh, Nina!' Gazing at the glossy printed image of the man she so recklessly loved, Anna burst into helpless tears. The face was so familiar, and so terribly and finally estranged from her. Nina sat on the bed, putting a sympathetic arm round her, murmuring, 'There, there!' and similar comforting phrases. She could not understand, Anna thought, or she would not offer comfort when there was none that could help things.

Presently she was calm enough to say, 'Nina, he leaves for Vienna sometime tonight. I have to see him before then — I have to explain — '

'But you are mad! You cannot see anyone — you are too ill!'

'I don't care! If I can't explain to him, then I don't want ever to be well again.'

'Oh, la la! Nonsense. But all the same, you are in love,' said Nina, trying to be fair. 'You are not in a reasonable state of mind. I will ring his flat for you and ask him to come.'

'Please. Or I must go to him.'

'That can't be allowed.' Nina was adamant. But when she had telephoned the theatre to get Baran's number, and then rang his flat, there was no reply. Several times in the next hour or two she repeated the call, meeting with similar lack of success each time. Anna, lying helpless in her bed, felt as though hope were ticking away with each passing minute. It was afternoon, and he was not there. Evening, James had said, was when he was due to leave. She couldn't let him go without seeing him. There was no reason with which she could support her passion; she could put forward no proof that what she felt was any more than a shallow and short-lived infatuation. All that mattered was what she felt, now; nothing else in the world seemed to matter but that. And she could not bear to let him go thinking that she had ruthlessly, unfeelingly used him. She would not make her reputation at his expense.

When Nina still had no reply from the flat, Anna at last sank back on her pillows, listless and drained of hope.

'Leave it, Nina,' she begged. 'It's no good now. He must have gone earlier, or maybe he's with Lensky, or — oh, anything at all.'

'You will stop worrying, then?'

'I'm too tired to go on worrying. I'll sleep for a while. But what about you? You've been here all day. You mustn't be a slave to my 'flu.'

'Well, I did promise that I would go and make tea for Sonya. She has the importunate Dr Davies to tea, and is in a state because she cannot decide if she will have him, and I have to go and make sensible conversation as well as the sandwiches. James said that he would come at six. Will you be all right until then? I have some orange juice ready for you in the kitchen. I'll get it.'

'Thanks. I'll be quite all right, don't worry. I shall sleep.'

'He will be told eventually, you know. And we can ask the First Lady to intercede for us. He will listen to her.'

'Yes,' agreed Anna, and thought of the ugly, compassionate face of Max Silbermann, and wondered how he could bear to watch his wife look with such love at another man. It was cruel, the hurt that people did to one another. Nor could one escape from it into dreams.

Nina left her at last, full of earnest directions as to what she should do if she found herself in need of anything. Anna waited for the sound of the door closing behind her; then, exercising all the self-control at her command, she waited a little longer. All was still. Her head throbbed in a dull, muffled kind of way, and her throat burned and her bones ached; nevertheless she must move, now, more quickly and stealthily than she had ever done in her life. When she was sure that Nina had really gone and would be thoroughly caught up in conversation downstairs, Anna very quietly sat up and wriggled to the edge of the bed. There, cautiously, she put her feet to the cold floor, and when her head was steadied again from its spinning she stood up, and began to collect together her clothes.

9

Miraculously, it seemed, Anna made her escape from the flat without attracting Nina's attention. She heard the sound of laughter from the Rodzinskas' flat as she passed the door, and hated herself for deceiving them, yet knew that she must do so.

She had never been to Heathrow Airport and did not know how best to get there. Reckless of cost, she hailed a taxi which was cruising hopefully in St Martin's Lane; she sank gratefully back into the dark, roomy interior of the cab, closing her eyes, not wanting to have to watch the long, tedious way across London. Her head still ached as though it would burst, and she felt weak and unsubstantial, as though she were somehow not quite real and might be only dreaming. But in a dream, surely, her head would not throb so and she would not feel so cold nor so burning hot.

She was confusedly aware of travelling out into a great wilderness of unrecognisable suburbs, up on to an elevated motorway which soared over rooftops, in among a sparse forest of tall tower blocks and out again on to a kind of plain where there were open fields and trees. Parents walked with their children in miniature parks, strolling contentedly in the waning light of late afternoon; it had been a fine day, and all was well with their world. There were horses standing in the fields, and people boating on a canal, all ordinary and happy as though there were nothing wrong at all. But then there wasn't, Anna thought, huddled and miserable; there was nothing to spoil their day, the cloud over the sun had been only in her mind. She ached more from apprehension than from fever. Where was she to look for him? And what was she to say to him, supposing that she did find him? What if he should, after all, blankly fail to understand her urgent agitation? It was, after all, still possible that she was only imagining the closeness that there had been between them, and that beyond annoyance he felt no particular distress at the publication of the pictures. They had met some three or four times in all; they had talked together only once. How could there be even the beginning of love between them? It didn't happen in life that way.

But a stubborn certainty that sometimes it did, supported Anna into the airport terminal building. Noise battered at her ears and dulled her understanding; the constant movement of people coming and going dazed her, made her feel lost and out of place. Everyone but she seemed to know just where they were going, chattering and clattering about the glass-walled concourse. The confusing background roar of jet engines somehow attached itself to Anna's headache as though she were producing it all inside her own skull.

She found her way up an escalator to the arrival and departure hall, which appeared to her to resemble something between a large swimming bath and a monster hotel foyer. There, helplessly, she looked around her. There were areas with seats, oases amid the restrained chaos, where people sat with expressions of resignation, some of them as though they expected to be there for a long time. There were higher levels of the concourse, and a great many doors leading heaven knew where. How was she to find Baran in all this? Would he even come here, or was there perhaps some separate and more elegant place for celebrities where they might come and go without having to rub shoulders with the herd? She had been mad to hope to find him here. He would never consent to travel like any common tourist.

At that moment he came into sight up the escalator, a fur coat over his arm, a travelling bag in his hand. She saw him before he caught sight of her, and all the breath seemed to be squeezed out of her body by one great spasm of feeling which made nonsense of all her doubts. It was a sense of total recognition, of passionate abandonment to a fate that could not be escaped — it was, simply, an admission by the whole of her being that she loved him.

He came to the top of the escalator, and stood for a moment looking about him as though he were about to walk onstage. It was a wholly unconscious attitude. He brought with him a sense of presence; his fine head, the flashing eyes, the splendid carriage, all set him apart from the crowd. Anna thought that he looked pale and finely drawn. People passing or sitting idly watching the world go by, seeing him, were curious, wondering, some recognising him and turning to their friends with nudges and nods, so that a little ripple of disturbance accompanied him as he moved forward into the concourse. For a moment Anna could not move, feeling as though she were the spectator of some play whose action meant everything to her and yet from which she was utterly barred. Then, somehow, she was walking towards him, praying that from somewhere she might find words to say to him, knowing that the last and most importance chance of her life had come and that all happiness depended on it.

He saw her. His step was checked; he stared at her as though she were some alien and hostile thing thrown into his path, a slow, cold anger beginning to burn in his eyes.

'What are you doing here?' he demanded harshly, all the contempt in the world in his tone.

'Please!' she begged, knowing that the tears stood in her eyes, not able to stop them. 'I have to explain. Please let me talk to you — just for a minute; it won't take more than that.'

He hesitated, looking at her with scarcely less anger, but considering.

'You came here only for this — to speak with me?'

'Yes. I tried to ring your flat, but — '

'Ah, the telephone is in another room. I was disinclined to answer, so I ignored it. The ringing does not disturb me.'

Typical, she thought; typically lofty unconcern for others.

'Let me explain to you,' was all she could say, weak, the tears ready to spill.

He took her by the arm and with unexpected decisiveness steered her past the bookstalls, the *bureaux de change*, the arrival gates, until they came to a quieter corner where there were empty seats. There they sat very close together on a bench by the wall. His hand remained on her arm, and seemed to burn through the thick wool of the jacket she was wearing, to close about the bone. She felt his nearness as though it flamed upon her skin, robbing her of breath. He was hard, vital, masculine, and awareness of him reduced her to incoherent, quivering helplessness. She could say nothing. Everything that she felt must surely be there in her eyes for him to read.

For a moment or two he searched her face as though he sought assurance of truth. Then he sighed, releasing her.

'You wanted to say — ?' The question was remote, polite, unpromising.

'About — about the photos. The *Sunday News*. You've seen them?'

'Yes. And I am not interested in apologies — nor in the information that of course if you had then known me you would not have done it.'

'But I didn't — I didn't send them to the paper. I would never have done anything with them.'

'Then why take them at all? Why spy on me in that peculiarly loathsome way?'

'Because you were there and you looked beautiful. I can't help taking pictures. I might as well ask you why you dance.'

He stared at her with a kind of perplexity, unwilling and yet half-believing. His face, so near to hers, was even now something she could not see without being dazzled by its beauty. He was magnificent and could never be otherwise. It wasn't fair. She trembled, feeling the heat of her fever burning her from within, and the nearness of him scorching her flesh, so that it seemed she must soon be consumed and nothing left of her but dying ashes. He must — before that he *must* understand and forgive her.

'I thought,' he said slowly, 'I thought that sometimes when we talked our minds were open to one another. I thought that you understood some things. Was that not so? Or did I dream — ?'

'Oh, no, it was real! Though I've wondered, too, if I dreamed it, because — because of who you are, because it seemed so unlikely.'

Looking at her in puzzled silence, slowly he shook his head.

'Then why did you give Lensky the means to punish me?'

'To punish you?'

'He resents my independence. He

would like to have me wholly bound to him — chained, a slave, a puppet. He is the fairground magician — his puppets have souls only at his command, extensions of his will, agents of his passion for the ballet. They are utterly his creatures. But I — I resist him, I go my own way; and so he resents me and looks for every chance to demonstrate what power he has. He displays me to the public as he would a doll, saying — 'See, this is my creature, this is what he is made of — see the sawdust, the painted tears — ''

'I didn't know! Oh, please believe that I didn't know!' Tears burst from her with as much passion as the words themselves carried. The pain of her aching head and her sore throat seemed all at one with the pain she felt at the wrong she had done him. 'James gave the pictures to Lensky,' she explained miserably. 'It was a sort of bribe, I suppose, so that he'd let me come and take pictures for the book. I'd only just taken them. You were standing on that little balcony — you looked — I don't know; it seemed to say so much about the loneliness of being famous, of having a great, isolating talent. And then you are magnificent to photograph just because of the way your features are arranged — even if you didn't dance, people would want to take pictures of you.'

'Farmer must have known what Lensky would do.'

'Maybe. I don't know; it was arranged so quickly, I didn't know what had hit me. I've never done anything like this before — I don't know the way things go.'

'Then you will be destroyed,' he said quietly, but with absolute conviction. 'You are in a world you do not know. I think you are truly innocent — and the innocent have no defences.'

'What can I do?' She wanted to fling herself into his arms, to beg him for protection and love; he was strong enough to carry all the burden of her inadequacies. But there still yawned between them the gulf made by his fame. He was not an ordinary man with whom one might reasonably safely fall in love. Anna began to shiver, suddenly cold although the air around her was warm. Baran looked more intently at her; abruptly he put the back of a hand to her brow and held it for a moment there, where it burned like ice upon her skin.

'You are ill!' he exclaimed, appalled. 'You are burning hot! You should be at home in bed, not here — '

'But I had to tell you, and you didn't answer the phone — '

'But how could I have known? And if I had known — See here, you will go home now, in a taxi, and go to bed.'

'But you do understand? You don't blame me now?' In her desperation she clutched at his hands, feverishly clasping and holding them. His grey eyes seemed to glitter, searching for some kind of certainty and not finding it; he shook his head.

'I don't know. How can I know

myself, or you? Forgiveness is not easy. I so passionately hate to be an object of curiosity, and then I cared that — but I will try to understand.'

'When you come back — ?'

'We shall see.' He closed her trembling, clutching hands up inside his own, holding them there in a moment's strong, certain tenderness. 'My life is very restless. There are few settled things in it, save for dancing. I am a dancer, and that is all. There's nothing more to me.'

'That's hard for a woman to believe,' she said, her voice very low.

'Exactly!' He smiled now for the first time; it was like winter sun, gleaming with pale, uncertain warmth. 'So you see how it is.'

'You must be free of encumbrances. Of course.' The words were like ashes in her mouth. But the hands holding hers gave them a little, impatient shake.

'No!' he said fiercely. 'You don't understand. Wait!'

But a shadow fell over them, lay

between them. Like a guilty child Anna looked up, and found herself gazing into the cold, speculative eyes of Vladimir Lensky.

'When I gave you the freedom of my theatre, Miss March, I did not intend that it should be extended so far.' The proud, bearded face was coldly angry, the hard obsidian eyes brooked no argument. He looked for a moment like an ancient Tsar of Russia, powerful and cruel.

'There was business to discuss,' Baran said, indifferently, releasing Anna's hands and rising to his feet. Anna rose too, stiffly, feeling the world dip and sway unsteadily about her. For a moment she clung to the hope that Baran would challenge Lensky about the publication of the photographs, but he said nothing, meeting her eyes when she turned to him with an uninterested look. Whatever he had been going to say to her was lost. He no longer cared.

She turned away, not even prompted by pride to assert herself.

'*Bon voyage*,' she said, and began to move away between the benches, the outstretched feet, the piles of luggage. Lensky followed her, laying a hand on her arm to restrain her for a moment. His fingers were very strong, white and fine; arrogant fingers, she thought, like the man himself.

'The photographs,' he stated bluntly, but with a note of distaste in his voice as though he could scarcely be troubled by such trivia.

'You never asked for my permission to publish,' she said, determined that her voice should not shake. 'I had to explain that.'

'Miss March, I did your career no small service by making those photographs available for publication. Are you not grateful? Had I asked your permission, would you not have given it?'

He waited for her to answer. She felt trapped, torn between the desire to think well of herself and the need to be honest.

'Yes,' she said at last, miserably. 'No. Oh — I don't know. How can I tell? I didn't know, then — '

'You had not then allowed yourself the folly of falling in love with one of my dancers. I warned you, did I not? Yet I thought it safe to take you at James Farmer's valuation. Evidently we are both mistaken in you.'

'James knows nothing about me,' she said flatly.

'How reckless, then, and how unstable your emotional affairs must be!' The cold, jet black eyes regarded her with the steady dislike and contempt of a moral man for the morally squalid. She felt that she had been summarily discarded. She could think of no defence; besides, the pain in her head was almost unbearable, so that she was as ready to weep from pain as from self-pity.

'You're not human!' she cried, quite losing control of her voice. 'You aren't human and you can't understand human weakness in others! You make a god of dancing and you sacrifice your dancers to it. You must be one of the most hated men on earth!' And she turned, shaking off his restraining hand, and went on unsteady legs across the concourse away from him. In doing so, for the first time she became aware of the presence of Tatiana Kirilova. The dancer stood apart from them, watching the little scene with a surprised and faintly amused expression. She was breathtakingly lovely; she brightened the air, like jasmine in a winter garden, her hair gleaming pale and golden, her face framed by a collar of soft, honey-coloured fur. Now, seeing Anna's awareness of her presence, she moved closer to Baran and lifted a delicately arched eyebrow at him, quizzical, assuming an immediate intimacy of understanding. 'These troublesome girls!' she seemed to say with that look. 'Poor darling!' Baran smiled back at her, took her long-boned, lovely hand and touched it to his lips; his grey eyes above her head sought Anna's and for a moment met her anguished gaze. She could not read what was in them, but it seemed to her like final dismissal. That was his world; a world of beautiful women who meant almost nothing, but were enough, occupying only just so much of his life as there was to spare from dancing. Anna had absolutely no place there at all.

She got somehow down the escalator and into a taxi, and directed it to take her back to Bloom Street. Tears rolled and rolled down her face and fell on to her hands; even though she closed her eyes they forced their way between the lids and fell. It was silly to weep so over something that couldn't be helped; it was foolish to cry for the moon when she had always known that it was out of reach. Even though she had crossed the dividing line between the real world and that magical, bright place of dreams, she had always been aware that the dividing line was there. Why, then, should she feel now as though her life was of no more use to her? It wasn't reasonable. But neither was love reasonable; she had contracted it like a sickness and felt ready to die of it. Silently and motionlessly she wept, letting the heavy tears fall until at last there seemed to be no more; but even then a rough sobbing from time to time caught at her breath and made her shudder, shaking her aching head and setting her teeth chattering as though she were cold.

Darkness had fallen by the time she reached Bloom Street. She paid off the taxi and laboured up the steep stairs to her flat, finding it as she had expected in a kind of muffled hysteria, James stalking up and down the hall in a fury, and Nina and her sister huddled miserably together in the sitting-room. In their relief at seeing her safe, they all turned on her in passionate reproach.

'You could get pneumonia! You weren't safe out! You should have told us at least where you had gone!'

'I thought you'd know,' was all she could say, weakly, not caring that they

236

must read in her tearstained face the failure of her mission.

'Anna — look — ' Helplessly, James put an arm round her, looking down at her with honest bewilderment and unhappiness that somehow touched her more deeply than anything he had ever done or said. For a moment she met his troubled eyes, seeing him contrasted with the magnificent, exotic beauty of Baran, the cold elegance of Lensky; he seemed by comparison with them utterly safe and wholesome and honourable. Perhaps, after all, it was James she should love; perhaps she was seeing things the wrong way round, mistaking unfamiliarity and excitement for true feeling, letting herself be carried away by glamour. Bruised and exhausted, feverish and muddled, she clung to him, buried her face in his shoulder.

'James — oh, James, I've made such a mess of things! You shouldn't have let me — you shouldn't have trusted me. I'm not safe near a theatre. I always wanted it so much — and to be so near something you terribly want, and yet not quite there, it's worse than never coming within miles! James, help me! Help me!'

'There, there! Oh, you poor infant — you're so ill! Look, come here, come back to bed. You ought never to have left it.'

'But you must help me.' She let him guide her through into the bedroom, sitting heavily down on the bed. 'James, give me something to belong to, something real that matters, so that I don't go chasing dreams any more.'

'You wanted to be free,' he reminded her. 'So that you could chase dreams.'

'I don't know what's good for me. You can see better than I can — you know what's real and what isn't.'

'Maybe.' He gazed at her in perplexity, his arm round her, a hand to her hair, stroking it with an unconscious soothing movement as one might comfort an unhappy child. Anna felt a passionate certainty that this was the most she had any right to expect of life. This was the best thing that could happen, to have someone there waiting with understanding, with gentleness to soothe away the weariness and the hurt of the world. She had not understood; she had never known a father to whom she could run like this with her childish pains. Not having a father to act as a pattern for the men in her life, she had not known what to look for — had gone after an illusion, a dream of mystery and excitement, when all the time something much more real had been to hand, waiting for her to recognise it.

Burning conviction of the rightness of this discovery seized her. She looked up at James, her eyes brimming with tears not now of misery but of an entirely new emotion.

'I was wrong,' she said. 'To want to be free, I mean. James, do you want to be engaged again?'

'Of course, yes. I'd never considered it really broken.'

'But — I mean — this time for real?'

'I'd never been sure that it wasn't,' he said gently. 'Yes — this time for real. Where's the ring?'

'On the chest of drawers, in that little dish.'

'Got it.' He came back now, and slipped the ring once more on to her finger. Very gently, with cool lips he kissed her burning forehead. 'There. We're engaged again. Now stop worrying and get back into bed. I shall ask Nina to send for Sonya's doctor again.'

He got up from the bed and stood for a moment looking down at her, his pleasant face full of concern and fondness. Her sight blurred; she swayed, and lay down, curling her legs up under her.

'Too tired . . . ' she said, and was asleep.

James went from the room and found Nina in the kitchen, squeezing oranges to make a drink.

'She fell asleep,' he said.

'Oh. Sonya has gone for Davies.'

There was a little silence.

'We're engaged again,' James at last said.

'Oh.' It was a very small sound. 'I congratulate you.'

'Thanks.' He wandered moodily over to the window. 'I must get her off the ballet and on to something different. Pity.'

'He will be away for over a week.'

'I suppose she may be fit enough to do a little more while he's away. We'll see. Why for God's sake do some men have this destructive power?'

'It's the power only of the lamp over the moth. One cannot blame the light because it burns the creature's wings. Poor moth!' said Nina, and went on fiercely squeezing oranges although all the juice had already come out of them.

10

As though her trip to the airport had somehow burned the fever out of her, Anna almost at once recovered. Before the week ended she was back at the theatre, trying to make the most of what time remained before Lensky and Baran should return. Daily class went on exactly as usual and rehearsals were supervised by the ballet mistress and the *répétiteur* just as carefully as though Lensky were there, watching with his cold, critical eyes. Anna photographed one more class and a rehearsal of *Spectre de la Rose*, with Krainov and Raimann dancing the roles made immortal by Karsavina and Nijinsky. There was rich material for pictures, and in some quite mechanical, unfeeling way Anna made the best of it, knowing that she had on film at the end of each session some fine shots, yet unable to feel any of the pride in them, the excitement and involvement she had felt for her previous work. It was as though such emotions had simply dried up in her.

She ought to have been able to feel at least some stirring of spirit at the extraordinary effect produced by the *Sunday News* pictures of Baran. Enquiries, requests, commissions came in a small avalanche. Quite suddenly a dizzying number of people wanted her to photograph them; agents of actors and singers besought her by telephone to portray this or that famous face in as interesting a light. In her numbed state of mind she would probably have ignored or declined all of these requests but for the determined energy of James and Nina, who together stood so close behind her that she could not begin to retreat. Between them they organised her into making an appointments book and then keeping such appointments as she made; they supervised the conversion of her sitting-room into a studio where she could take indoor portraits, importing spotlights and reflectors and rolls of background paper, suitable chairs and smaller props such as hats, fans, feather boas and the like, in which Nina took a great delight. Numbly, Anna suffered herself to be propelled through all these motions, and was blankly dismayed at her own lack of feeling. She wanted to share in Nina's enthusiasm, yet could not do so; she felt as though some deep wound had severed all the nerves by which she would normally experience such emotions. It was not her fault that she could not feel any joy, and yet the lack of it made her guilty and reinforced her wretchedness.

Marcia Blaise took her aside after the class which she photographed that week. The First Lady led her by the hand into her dressing-room, a carpeted cell with bare walls and a huge mirror fringed by naked bulbs, with great baskets of flowers standing in the corners, filling the air with an oddly funereal perfume, reminding Anna suddenly of Midhampton cemetery, her mother's grave heaped with wreaths already dying. Anna sat as she was bidden in the one comfortable chair, looking at all the cards and telegrams stuck round the mirror and taped on to the wall, thinking it strange that someone so pre-eminently successful as Blaise should still so naïvely follow theatrical custom. Surely at such a level one didn't still crave the reassurance of first night good wishes? Yet, the greater the eminence, the greater the possible fall — maybe, after all, one needed every support one could get. Self-confidence must never be allowed to falter; one moment's hesitation for a dancer must mean disaster.

'I wanted to speak to you about Alexei,' the First Lady said simply, sitting at the dressing-table with her back to Anna so that they watched one another through the mirror; it seemed somehow easier than looking directly at one another. Anna's hands locked fiercely into each other.

'What about him?' she asked thinly.

'There was some understanding between you — or perhaps a misunderstanding. Something. And it has made you unhappy. I want your happiness. Also I want his — more perhaps than anything in the world. I have everything else. How can I use what influence I have with him, so as to make both of you happy?'

'I don't know. I don't know what's for the best at all, or if there's any way you could help. I'm engaged to James, anyway.'

'But not very securely? Max told me — '

'Oh.' Anna remembered her conversation with Max Silbermann in the bar at the Festival Hall. It seemed a very long time ago that she had told him she did not love James. 'Things have changed,' she said, helpless to explain. 'I've decided, now, that after all I do want to marry James.'

Marcia Blaise looked at her through

the mirror. The dancer's eyes seemed to grow enormous in her delicate head, and her face all at once showed her age, dry and tired, the skin papery; her whole frame seemed to shrink and slacken. Anna's own reflection looked by comparison flat and stolid, uncomprehending eyes in a puddingy, pale face, a mulish set to her jaw.

'I am sorry,' the First Lady said, her voice very low. 'I had such hopes — '

'Don't hope. Anyway, it wouldn't have worked. He's not of my world, nor am I of his. I shan't see him again. I've done almost all the work I can do here.'

'So quickly?'

'There are other companies to be covered. Besides, Lensky — '

'Is he the trouble between you and Alexei?'

'No. Really, the barrier is mostly just that he doesn't want me; he made it very clear. And then, the unreality of it all — '

'I don't see anything unreal in it.'

'You don't know me — you don't

know Anna March from Midhampton.'

'But you are no longer — '

'I am. I always will be. My father left my mother, so early in my life that I don't remember him. I can only remember how unhappy she was and how insecure we felt. I want, if I ever marry, to marry someone very safe — someone I don't love too much, so that if I should lose him it won't hurt more than I can bear. And that's James. If I — if ever I let myself love, want — the other one — I'd never again know any peace.'

There was a silence. Marcia Blaise looked at her through the mirror with huge dark eyes in which it seemed to Anna that she could see tears deep down like a great well.

'And he?' the dancer said at last. 'What of him? What of his happiness?'

'I can't believe that it depends on me. He wants to travel alone — he said so. He can't ever love a woman as he loves the dance. His life is built on uncertainties . . .'

'Do you not yet know, Anna, that people sometimes say what isn't strictly true, in an attempt to excuse what they know themselves to lack? His need for love, like yours, is so strong, so hungry that he daren't give in to it. He fears pain as much as you do. He fears not being able to love enough, because he knows the demands of his life, and can't imagine a woman who could love him despite all that.' Helplessly she shrugged. 'You must *think*, Anna! Don't shut your eyes because of fear.'

'But James — '

'For his sake, too! Could you make him really happy?'

'He must think so, mustn't he?'

Marcia sighed and closed her eyes. Anna felt guilty and obstinate, and thoroughly wretched. James was her sanctuary; since her fever and her abandonment of hope then, she had clung to him as if he were the one safe refuge in her life. He was understanding and kind, and didn't make a fuss over things; he was all she had. Without him she was nothing — certainly not the suddenly fashionable Anna March, photographer. She had to marry him now.

Again she assured Marcia Blaise of this, begging her to forget that there had ever been anything at all between her and Baran.

'He's not of my world,' she insisted. 'Maybe James is second best now, but in the long run he'll prove to have been the best choice.'

But Blaise clearly did not agree, and Anna was left feeling that she had by her obstinacy alienated a friend.

There were still some photographs to be taken about the theatre, the façade, the foyer, the auditorium, stage hands and doormen, wardrobe rooms and scenery dock, and the stage itself in its daytime aspect of bare boards and hanging canvas. These were soon done, leaving Anna with no excuse for going into the Imperial again. Ahead of her lay weeks with the Royal Ballet, the Festival Ballet, the Ballet Rambert; then there were to be sessions with orchestras, with opera companies and theatre companies; there were growing numbers of private commissions, portraits of intoxicatingly important people. Anna tried to turn her attention to these activities, and found rather to her surprise that gradually a certain warmth of feeling did come back to her; she was interested despite herself, the fascination of the work pulling against her faintly guilty feeling that if she had truly loved Baran she would never again experience such straightforward pleasure in living. After all, perhaps one did not actually die of love.

She became excited over the visual possibilities of music, discovering that someone playing an instrument with concentration and passion could be quite as interesting to watch as a dancer or an actor. Several of her best pictures found their way into the *Sunday News*, and others into the daily Press, until without ever having intended it she found that she was being drawn into a certain circle of London's social and artistic life where everyone was celebrated or notorious for something, where all the names were sooner or later to be encountered on the gossip pages of the papers. It was a section of society in which James was already comfortably at home. To her astonishment Anna found that not only had she the entrée into this glittering world and the right to drop its prestigious names quite freely, but that her own name was currently as much in use as any; Anna and James took their place on the lists of people to be invited to any self-respecting party in Kensington or Chelsea, Hampstead or Islington, or even Barnes and places further flung.

'Do you suppose that I could consider myself one of the jet set?' she asked James one day over an unusually quiet lunch at her flat. They had just been presented by Nina with the *Express*, in which the diarist had duly noted their presence at Lady Georgina Dewey's ball the night before, with a rather bad photograph, flashlit, in which they both clutched champagne glasses and looked extremely dissipated. 'I've never actually been in a jet plane. Or in any kind of plane, come to that.'

'How frightful! We must repair the omission. Paris?'

'Marvellous! A weekend in Paris — just the thing to establish us as jet set and fashionable in our morals.'

It was an incautious thing to have said, and she at once regretted it. Certainly she was engaged to James; that was quite decided, and because they were both somehow nervous of the whole business it was an engagement all the more fiercely binding. But beyond that their relationship was uncomfortably ill-defined. Once she had recovered from the violent fever that had made her so ill, and was more like herself again, James had taken the necessary step between them to make their engagement something more like a promise of marriage between people in love; one night, after a trip to the cinema to see an improving but rather gloomy Swedish film, he had gathered her against him in the taxi taking them home and had kissed her — cautiously at first, as though for him it was something of an experiment, as though he were still far from certain of how she felt about him. What she most felt was gratitude, liking, affection, and though none of these even remotely approached the intensity of passion she had experienced when Alexei Baran kissed her, yet they were warm and good feelings, making it possible for her to respond convincingly to James' kisses even though they were only second best. But a certain reserve remained; like a well of shadow between them lay the knowledge that despite all affection and good-will they were not deeply in love. They would marry eventually rather as a couple might have married centuries ago, the match made for them by careful families, positively knowing only that they did not actually dislike one another. Sometimes when Anna looked into the future she felt afraid of the long and arid years that she saw there.

Now, on the subject of Paris, she said, 'But shouldn't we wait until spring? Or is Paris worth seeing even in November?'

'It's worth seeing at any time of year. We'll go to the opera, the ballet — the theatre, too, if your French is up to it.'

It was very casually settled. Anna then forgot all about it until almost the eve of their flight, when Nina stood over her and made her sort out what clothes she would take and what she could use the occasion as an excuse to buy. Her wardrobe had grown considerably since her first panic rush to the boutique round the corner. She had become accustomed to using clothes as a kind of disguise, knowing that if she looked a part she would be able to play it adequately — and feeling that almost all of her life now demanded that she play a part. For Paris she decided on the most deceptively casual and expensive of her trouser suits, and an evening dress or two, with the fur she had recently bought and still wore with a secret sense of guilt at the cost of it.

'You will buy dresses in Paris,' Nina declared. 'To go to Paris and to buy nothing would be madness. How I envy you!' She expressed total desolation. Anna sensed beneath the banter a real unhappiness; Nina had said nothing, but there was a preoccupied air about her sometimes, a diminution of vitality which made Anna wonder whether despite all her worldliness the girl had allowed herself to fall in love with someone. Nothing was said, and Anna could not feel that she had the right to pry, being no longer of the theatre — for doubtless it was one of those virile and glorious young men in the *corps de ballet*, and Nina had now to face the choice between Lensky's company and love . . . But then, Anna reflected bitterly, one could live despite the denial of love. She herself was proof of it. Nina would doubtless take account of this, and survive.

Heathrow Airport with James seemed a different place from that in which Anna had talked to Baran. Involuntarily she looked at the place where they had sat together; a family sat there now, spread all over the benches, a fat baby smearing chewed rusk on to the seat. She tried not to feel pain clutching at her when she remembered; that was all done with, there was nothing to be gained by remembering. She had not been near the theatre since his return and Nina had been careful not to mention him, so that there was nothing to remind her either of his rejection or of his kiss, nor even of his existence — save for the fact that she could not rid her mind of the image of his face, of the proud bones, the winged brows, and those grey eyes that so mysteriously burned between black lashes. Now she was filled again with the ache of his leaving her, longing gnawed at her until she was feverish with pain and with the desire to get away from this place, to flee his ghost. She let James pilot her through Customs and at last on to the plane, and was too much preoccupied with her own unhappiness to realise that she had become at last genuinely airborne in the manner necessary to her standing in fashionable society.

Jet travel, she decided when at last she wearily turned her attention to it, was not particularly exciting. One might almost be in a superior kind of coach, but with less interesting scenery outside the window; there was too much cloud for more than fragmentary glimpses of the far-away ground. But it was at least quick. They were amazingly soon in Paris, with the evening of Thursday and a four-day weekend in front of them. At such a prospect the spirits of even the most lovesick must rise. It was with quickened pulse and a livelier eye that Anna looked out of the window on the round-about cab drive from Orly into the city.

Paris was strangely like all her mental

images of it, and yet again strangely different. The elegant grey stone buildings, the tree-lined boulevards, the window shutters and awnings and speeding traffic were all as she had imagined, and the Eiffel Tower, Nôtre Dame and the Seine looked just as they should, yet there was a feeling of unexpected similarity to London, something, some likeness such as perhaps all great Western cities have to one another, so that she could not feel that she had come so very far from home.

Their hotel, not very far from the Opéra, was luxurious in the traditional manner, more Claridges than Hilton, throwing Anna into a small panic of uncertainty about how one used the facilities of such a place. She had never stayed in an hotel in her life before. James, in the room adjoining hers, was entirely at home, and put her mind to some extent at rest.

'Simply assume that the place belongs to you, and that they are all morons of an infinitely lower station in life. Everything's for the asking at the other end of a telephone; your whim is law.'

Anna could not be convinced that her veneer was that hard yet; however, she was comforted by his assurances and his nearness, so much so that she resolved to leave the door between their rooms open as it now stood, at least until bed-time. She trusted James.

Her room was all terra-cotta frills and flounces, just like the décor in a Feydeau farce; the ornate pink-and-gold bed was well sprung, there was a pretty writing desk before the long voile curtains of the window, and the carpet was deliciously soft underfoot. Her own bathroom opened from the bedroom, and here all was sumptuous green and pink marble, with golden dolphin taps. There was time now for a bath before they went out to the opera; Anna ran the water and poured perfumed oil lavishly into it, and sank gratefully into its scented warmth, wondering why for all its speed jet travel should make one feel so extraordinarily tired. She could understand now for the first time why musicians and dancers who flew constantly around the world should feel such strain, becoming exhausted merely by the demands of continual movement. Airports, hotel rooms, theatre dressing-rooms . . . thus Baran had summed up the greater part of his life. She understood, now, his lack of delight in travel. Where would he be just now, at this moment, as she was thinking of him?

As swiftly as the thought came she banished it, punishing herself by climbing out of the bath and standing under a cold shower. She would *not* think of him! She had come to Paris with James, and she would not think at all of the man with whom she would so much rather be. At least with James she could look forward to a calm sort of weekend.

She dressed for the evening in flame velvet, halternecked and somehow very Parisian, though she had never thought it so before. Her hair she knotted up on the crown of her head. She had discovered that a certain simplicity and lack of ornament suited her best, making an advantage of her height and giving her a look of distinction. How very near she came to a real and rare beauty was something of which she had no awareness, nor had she any idea of how much the success she currently enjoyed had to do with it; nevertheless she no longer felt plump and plain, no longer wanted to hide herself away from critical eyes. James approved, and she had confidence in his taste.

Tonight particularly she wanted to please him. She had an uneasy feeling of being here under false pretences. A weekend in Paris was for lovers; there ought to be magic and romance in it, there ought to exist at least the possibility of passion, of recklessness and self-forgetting. Did he expect anything more from her than the amiable companionship that normally bound them? She could not imagine that kisses lukewarm in London were likely to become any warmer in Paris, and felt guilty because she could not think so, as though she were wilfully planning to disappoint him.

Their seats were booked at the Opéra; they walked, since it was not far, through wide, bright and restless thoroughfares, the night air cool but soft against their faces. Paris at night made a different sound from London — a more lively, a somehow more southern sound. The Opéra was glittering and splendid, very much an evening-dress affair. They were to see the first night of a new production of *Salomé*, and clearly they were in company with most of fashionable theatre-going Paris. From their seat in the stalls they could see all round the theatre. Anna unashamedly craned her neck; at some distance from them she had already seen and waved at one actress she had recently photographed, and a young man who haunted the Martineaus' Kensington house. James was able to point out to her this and that writer, a film director, a diplomat. There was a general dazzle of lights, jewels, a heavy mixture of perfumes; conversation in French sounded somehow a great deal more witty, and sometimes very much more coarse, than the same kind of chatter would have sounded in English. Anna settled into her comfortable seat with a little sigh of contentment; it was all novel enough to be interesting, and at the same time familiar so that she felt really quite at home. She would enjoy this evening . . .

Just two rows in front of her, as the lights began to go down, a couple arrived, late but magnificently unhurried as though they had every assurance that the performance would not start without them. Reflected light from the curtain, from the orchestra pit, silhouetted them, shining on the woman's gleaming hair and satiny bare shoulders, on her companion's rough raven locks, glancing off his high cheekbones and straight nose, emphasising the perfect, imperious moulding of his face. Anna's breath was caught in her chest, and a pain began there and remorselessly spread out through every limb, a slow, heavy ache of recognition and despair. Baran and Kirilova! How could it be that they should have come here on this night of all nights?

James beside her restively stirred, and then took her hand in his and squeezed it.

'Damn!' he said softly. 'Sorry, darling, but . . .'

'It doesn't matter — really, it doesn't matter.' But he must surely know from her trembling and from the tightness of her voice that it did matter. The lights died, the music began, and Anna could do nothing but watch in fascination the line of light along Baran's profile, the perfect immobility of his head. He watched the stage and listened with perfect impassivity; one could not tell whether in fact he saw or heard anything at all, so utterly without movement or expression did he sit. But when the interval came and the lights were brought up, unhurriedly and deliberately he turned and looked back as though he had felt her gaze upon him, and met Anna's fascinated and unhappy eyes. For a long, devastated moment they looked at one another. She felt that he saw directly into her soul, whereas she saw nothing but the dark, fierce grey of his wonderful eyes; she wanted to cry out to him, to make some frenzied plea for his understanding and his love, she wanted to weep for him and claim him, to make him somehow perceive that their destiny was together, that her passion was no shallow, ephemeral thing, but the whole of her being on fire with love.

That much, if he could read it, was in her eyes for him to see. Then Kirilova turned, too, following the direction of his intent gaze. She recognised Anna at once; the flicker of understanding and of distaste in her eyes was unmistakeable. She murmured something in Baran's ear, and laughed; he after a moment relinquished Anna's gaze and looked into Kirilova's lovely face, and he too laughed. He turned his back on Anna and did not look at her again.

She sat somehow through the rest of the opera, hearing it as a dreadful screeching noise in the background of her tormented thoughts. It was a relief to get to the end, to rise and await her chance to escape. All the same, in the foyer they were so much detained by the slow movement of the crowd and then by the young actress, who insisted on introducing them to her companion, that Baran and Kirilova overtook them. Once more Anna suffered the fire of his scornful eyes. He very faintly inclined his head, unable out of politeness to do less; his eyes went from Anna to James, and then to her left hand on which the ring of garnets and pearls hung heavy and richly glowing against her white skin. Again he met her eyes, and this time it seemed to her that there was contempt in them as well as rejection.

She was saved from tears by anger,

by the thought that he had no right to despise her for taking what happiness was offered by James when he himself had denied her the only love that might make her truly happy. He wanted, he said, to travel alone. That might be all very well for him, encompassing such diversions as the beautiful Kirilova. But for Anna such a life apart was not possible. She wanted love — needed to be loved, to feel secure in someone's admiration and affection. And to fill such a need James would do very well. Baran had no right to resent her choice of compromise.

Thus upheld by anger, she was able to turn her back on Baran this time before he had a chance to so dismiss her. When she looked round again he had gone. She did not see him again in Paris, though the memory of having seen him and of how she still felt about him overcast the whole of the weekend and effectively killed any faint stirrings of the romantic spirit.

11

Meeting Baran in Paris had the effect of making Anna more than ever certain that she must marry James, and soon — rather as though in her heart she feared that delay might give her time to change her mind.

'It needn't make much difference to the way we live,' she pointed out to him. 'I can keep this flat on as a studio — it's ideal for the purpose.'

'Shall I ever see anything of you at my place?' His smile was rueful. 'Perhaps I'd do better to move in here.'

'Or we can get somewhere altogether new, if you'd rather.' She looked round the room where they were sitting, at the aubergine walls, the white shelves, the photographic lamps and the paper rolls on their tall stands dwarfing everything near them. She would be loth to leave this flat; it was home to her now, she had grown fond of it. And there across the road was the great shell of the Imperial casting its shadow on the front of the house — and inside the shell, somewhere, sometimes, was Baran. It was as near to him as she could come.

She ought not on the eve of marriage to James to be thinking so, and it worried her and made her unreasonable.

'You aren't going to be jealous of my work, I hope?' she demanded now, irritably. 'I do intend to go on with it.'

'Darling, of course you will, and I'm not, really, not jealous. Only, perhaps, a little wary. I'm not sure that emancipated modern marriages are as satisfying as one would hope. There should be more to it than a couple of quite separate lives put side by side.'

'It's a bit late to worry about that. Would you rather call it off? You don't have to marry me just because — '

'Because of what?' He looked at her and smiled, and then shrugged, sighing. 'Oh, don't let's quarrel.'

'No. Don't let's quarrel.' Anna got up from the sofa and went to the window, looking out at the dark hump of the theatre which crouched there like a vast tortoise shell on the ground. She didn't want to quarrel with James; it wasn't safe to do so. All the same, the thought stirred within her that perhaps a quarrel might be a good thing — that possibly there were fears in both their minds that could only be liberated by an outright quarrel. But they were civilised people, she and James; civilised people do not squabble. And so her fears stayed locked up in her head, and the time of their marriage at Christmas drew near.

Helen Martineau, curiously enough, was more ruthless and effective in presenting Anna's doubts to her so that she could not evade them. The conductor's wife, from hardly disguised contempt, had come round to an attitude of indulgent patronage once it was quite clear to her that, whether she approved or not, Anna was going to be a success. She had insisted that Anna must visit her studio; she had even taken photographs which despite Anna's instinctive mistrust of the intention behind them had turned out well, presenting a girl with an obstinate face, hard and determined looking and yet somehow haunted by a kind of rejected dreaming, a strange, smothered wistfulness which might have softened the features into beauty.

'You're very calm about this marriage of yours,' Helen said to her one day only a week and a half before the date set for it. They were in Helen's studio, the top floor of the tall mansion which she and Martineau occupied. From here there was a dreamy view of Kensington and Chelsea rooftops, a vast sea of affluence upon the crest of which it seemed natural for Helen to float. She had all the self-assurance in the world; she made Anna feel no more than an unfledged child.

'Ought I to be excited?' Anna retorted now. 'I thought it rather juvenile to make a fuss.'

'Nonsense! You're calm about it because you feel nothing.' Helen sat on a red plush sofa, on a dais against a white backdrop, where she was accustomed to pose sitters for portraits. She was a very striking woman — glamorous and interesting, Anna thought, rather than beautiful; she was a trifle too heavy, too hard and forceful to be really beautiful, yet she could convince one that she had beauty by the very intensity of her own will to do so. 'I know James,' she was saying now. 'I've known him for years. I don't want to see him wasted on the wrong woman.'

'Really, you haven't the least right to assume — '

'I'm not assuming. I know. Come on, now — admit it. You aren't very much in love with him, are you? Not so that you burn and ache with it — not so that life without him would be grey and grotesque?' Helen's smile was sceptical, cynical; steadily she watched Anna, waiting for the admission that she knew must come.

'No,' said Anna reluctantly, feeling the truth dragged from her. 'I don't love him like that. But there are other ways of loving.'

'Little idiot!' The words were spat out with real violence, startling and momentarily quite frightening Anna. Astonished, she stared at Helen, her heart thudding and her face flooded with colour.

'What?' she timidly said. 'I don't — I — '

'You know the other kind of love, don't you? The kind that matters, the real thing — and yet you'd marry James with some luke-warm sisterly affection for him, and hope to be happy?' Scorn blazed out of the woman's eyes. 'And who is it you really love? What of him? What's he to do when you're miserable and out of reach?'

'He's not — there's nothing at all in it.'

'There can be anything in it you

choose, if you've the will to make things go your way.' As if despite herself, Helen Martineau's glowing eyes turned to a photograph that hung on the studio wall — the only picture visible in the whole room, and one that dominated it, of Zoltan Szabo, the concert pianist. Anna recalled rumours she had heard of a passionate and interestingly doomed affair between these two, and then remembered contradictory rumours of no affair at all, of a past affair, of every combination of involvement from love to hatred.

'I don't know that I have that much will,' she said. 'Or that it would be good for me to try to impose my will on events. I want to be reasonably happy and secure. I shall be so with James.'

'Secure!' Helen Martineau laughed derisively. 'Oh, well — if that's what you want! But happy — do you really believe that happiness is only the absence of pain? Good God, girl, happiness *is* a pain! You can't know that you're ecstatically happy without feeling the pain of intense emotion. That's inseparable from the experience.'

'Maybe I'm a coward, then. Or a temperate person, not made for extremes.'

'Rubbish! With your face — '

'My mother loved my father. She suffered for it all her life after he left us.'

'So you'll play safe and try not to love. But it's too late, isn't it? Tell me,' said Helen, suddenly inspired, 'is it Baran? Oh, of course — don't bother to deny it, I can see, I can feel your pulse beat in the air. So — you really love Alexei Baran. You love him so much that you're ready to die of it, and yet you'd marry poor James out of some incredible notion that he can make you happy. Poor infant! And poor, poor James! Oh, you ought to think of him!'

And for the first time Anna did so, with a real effort of honesty. She knew so little about James. He was almost as much a stranger to her still as Carlos Martineau, whom she watched at lunch as the three of them ate together in the

Martineaus' elegant dining-room, fancying that she saw in his gentle, remote kind of courtesy and his wistfulness a foreshadowing of what James might become, unhappily tied to her. It was well enough known that the Martineaus lived almost apart from one another. If Helen loved Szabo, and still turned towards him from the prison of her marriage, the parallel was complete. That was how it would be with herself and James.

She would have liked to tell Nina about it, to have talked it over with her, but Nina was still preoccupied by whatever trouble of her own was gnawing at her, making her remote and draining her of vitality. It somehow made a barrier between them, preventing Anna from quite finding the courage to ask what was wrong; neither could she pour out her own problems in the hope of being understood and advised in Nina's frank and Continental way. And all the time the thought secretly ticked away, a little packaged explosive in her mind which could blow all the rest to smithereens, that he, Baran, was not so far away, that after all if she really wanted to she could see him; no one would stop her if she walked into the theatre one morning; she could go to a class, wait by the door, stop him as he came out . . .

Over and over again she pictured it in her mind, tormenting herself with the impossible dream, pretending that the power to decide lay in her own hands. In fact he would certainly reject her, and she knew it, and yet continued to dream.

One day, not having done so since before the trip to Paris, she went past the front of the theatre and deliberately stopped to look at the display photographs there. Some of them were of Blaise and Baran in *Les Sylphides*; she had taken them herself. Standing in front of the doors, looking into the mysterious crimson darkness of the foyer, Anna felt tears rush to her eyes and a sob rise in her throat; she hurried blindly home, not able to bear the misery of her own loneliness and yet able to see nothing in the future but that same private hell of loneliness stretching on and eternally on, shut out from all that might have made living worth while.

She tried to work hard, to forget her own problems in the technical challenge presented by photographing musicians in the depressing gloom of the Festival Hall by rehearsal lighting. Despite herself, she enjoyed photographing Martineau; there was a puppyishness, an unselfconscious eagerness which showed itself when he conducted music that he loved and when it was going well. She longed to photograph the magnificent Szabo, but caught him in a perverse mood, and after one annihilating glare from his fine eyes she dared not argue her case. He was clearly in his world what Baran was in the ballet. She could understand why Helen Martineau might love him to the point of madness; he had, as Baran had, the kind of passionate, vital arrogance which demanded that one either adore or utterly reject him. Both stood in lordly isolation quite apart from the common run of men. Yet someone — quite an ordinary girl, by all accounts — had been rash enough to marry this one. Anna could not believe that she did not regret it almost every day of her life. How could any woman feel safe with such a man? No — she had done the right thing, she had chosen James, who was ordinary and safe and would never make her utterly wretched, though he might never make her ecstatically happy either. She would not, as Szabo's wife must have done, mistake a brief delirium for the promise of lasting bliss.

But after that, when she compared James with Szabo — with him because he was more bearable to think of than Baran — she felt chilled and small, and wanted to weep.

Going back to her flat after a morning spent with Carlos and the

280

orchestra, she let herself in quietly, moving with the slow, careful precision that comes sometimes from the exhaustion of emotions. James had said that he might come to lunch; she was not surprised to hear his voice from the kitchen, together with that of Nina, both above the gentle hiss of something frying on the cooker. They were deep in conversation and had not heard her come in.

Standing in the hall, her camera bag still in her hand, Anna was caught all at once by a strange, unexpected note of intensity in the murmuring voices. She became very still, straining her ears to catch what was said, conscious of no dishonour in doing so but rather of a great urgency.

Nina's voice was very low, muffled as though there were something in the words which even the speaker feared to make clear.

'God, what *are* we to do?' was James' response, in tones of a desperate pain such as Anna had never heard in his voice before. 'So near — I can't go back on it! What ought we to do?'

'I ought to have spoken sooner, or not to have spoken at all,' Nina then said, her voice choked with tears. 'But I thought that I could keep it a secret. I did not know that love could be so savage!'

'And I all the time thought that it was only on my side, and would pass as these fancies do. It's not our fault, little one. How could we help it?'

'What are we to do, James? If you go on and marry — '

'We shall all be miserable. I know. I shall have to tell her. It isn't as though she deeply cares for me; I've never convinced either of us of that.'

'I should be the one to tell — '

'No — not you. I must. Oh, damn Baran — !'

'Ah, he is madder and sadder than all of us. But he is dedicated. Somehow he evades love. James, I hate myself — I ought to go away — '

Anna did not wait to hear any more.

Very softly, and with her heart beating so loudly that it deafened her to everything else, she crept back to the door and let herself out on to the landing. Standing there, her head pressed against the shiny panels of the door, she silently shook with bitter laughter. James and Nina! So that was the reason for Nina's recent quietness and her absence from the upstairs flat! Anna felt that she must have been blind, selfish and stupidly blind, not to have seen what was happening. Nina and James had fallen in love, and she, immured in her own absorbing miseries, had not even noticed.

It was beyond tears; the only possible response seemed to be laughter, but of a kind that she had seldom known before. At last, making a great deal of unnecessary noise, she re-entered the flat, and was some time going into the kitchen, so that when she did so all was innocently in order and there was nothing to confirm what she had overheard save for the way Nina and

James did not look at one another.

After a rather quiet lunch, she sent them both away, pleading the necessity of work. They went reluctantly, as though the very fact of being handed a period of unexpected freedom in one another's company made them feel guilty. She ought to have seen, she told herself helplessly — it was so obvious that only the most blind and stupid observer could fail to see it. There was a compulsion between the two of them such as there had never been and could never be between herself and James. Her only problem was to decide how she should deal with the situation now that she knew.

One obvious course seemed open to her, and she took it. She ran away. It was perhaps cowardly, and certainly it was undignified, but she could think of nothing else that she could bear to do. She hastily cancelled such appointments as could be dealt with over the phone, packed a suitcase and her camera bag, and caught the first possible train to Midhampton. There she might be able to see things in some kind of perspective and so work out what she was to make of the mess her life had got into. She left a message for James and Nina, not telling them where she had gone but making it sufficiently clear that the marriage was at least postponed, and saying that she had to be alone for a while to think.

Midhampton seemed very small and scruffy and friendly. It was a blunt, comfortable Midland market town, reasonably prosperous, cheerfully existing without much in the way of arts or culture, but full of ordinary, down-to-earth people. Anna's old landlady, Mrs Baines, was thrilled to see her and readily offered her a room for as long as she should want it. 'Not your old one, love, but the one Mrs H had — she went and died, you know, not on the premises, I'm happy to say, but in the General, ever so quick. It's all nice and aired and ready for you to step into.'

Anna explained her need of a break

in terms of fatigue and over-work.

'Oh, I daresay! And fancy you getting into the papers! We keep on seeing bits about you — quite a name you're making for yourself. Mind you, I always did think you'd get on in life — just like young James Farmer. Do you know, I remember him when he joined the *Gazette*, when he was nothing more than a boy? Such a way he had with him, even then. And are you going to marry him as the papers say?'

'I haven't quite decided,' said Anna untruthfully. In fact, her mind was quite made up. She would marry no one. James must be free to marry Nina; she was too fond of both of them to contemplate anything else. Looking at it in that way, she discovered that her feeling for both of them was remarkably similar — she was fond, she had affection. But she could not feel for James anything more intense. Clearly it would have been wrong to have married him, from whatever hopes of security and contentment; she must clear her head of all such delusions and start again, trying to see the world with more adult and self-reliant eyes, not reaching out after a settled, safe existence just because she was lonely and feared the future.

All the same, it was easier to think these things than to live through them. She wandered about Midhampton with a preoccupied and lost sensation, looking in blank unrecognition at the town she knew so well, wondering through a thick mental fog how it was she came to be there; sometimes it seemed that this was a dream, and sometimes London was the dream and this the reality. The memory of Baran tormented her, haunted her; she went over and over in her mind every moment they had shared, every word, every look. There were few enough such moments. Whatever the feeling between them, it had sprung instantly, spontaneously into being, owing nothing to time or to familiarity; it had received little enough encouragement. Longing still burned within her and would not for one second let her forget that she had met and loved him, and could never again be as she had been before. She had no means of knowing whether he even so much as remembered her existence, but feared that he did not. He, after all, was a dancer — his genius devoured all his energy and left none for loving or for vain regret.

It was necessary that she should do something positive to release James from their engagement. After three days she wrote to him, saying simply that she had realised that to marry him could make neither of them happy. It seemed enough; it was not by now even a very difficult letter to write. She put her address on it, feeling that now things were settled there was no need to conceal her whereabouts; he had a right, anyway, to be able to get in touch with her if he wanted to. But it was not James who replied to the letter. At once, by return post, a communication came from Max Silbermann.

'Dear Anna,' it said, 'I am sure that you will forgive my asking for you. Marcia is ill. There has been some fear of it for a long time. She will probably recover perfectly well, but she wants to see you. It would be a great relief to me if you could come.'

It was like a blow, a physical blow accompanied by a reproach. So great had been her resolve to keep away from anywhere Baran might be that she had deserted her friends in the ballet. For weeks she had seen nothing of Marcia Blaise. What was the illness? When nothing definite was specified, one always automatically assumed the worst. In a flurry of fear and self-condemnation, she packed what she might need and took a train south once more, impatient to be there; she went directly from the main line station in London to Richmond, where Max and Marcia lived by the river.

The day was grey and cold; the river lapped against the landing-stage at the foot of the garden, deep and sluggish and unfeeling. Everything within the house was very still. Anna was ushered in by the housekeeper to a room overlooking the garden, where Max almost at once came to her, taking her hands in his and kissing her on the cheek.

'Dear Anna, I so hoped that you would come! She has some notion that she ought to have talked to you more about Alexei. You will not find this too difficult?'

'No,' said Anna, her heart lying heavy and cold like lead within her. 'But there's nothing to be done, even for her.'

'Give her the comfort of knowing that she has tried, eh? She worries so about him.'

'Because she loves him.'

Max Silbermann smiled, and when he smiled thus one forgot the ugliness of his round little face and saw only the understanding in his eyes.

'Because she loves him, but not quite enough — and because he loved her, and that is no longer enough, either.'

'Oh.' Anna felt helpless, inexperienced and gauche. 'I — is she very ill? Can I go to her?'

'There is pneumonia. But the worst is over; with rest she will eventually be well, though she may not dance again — there will always be a weakness of the lungs.'

She may not dance again — a small, inadequate phrase to express the end of so much. Shown up to the dancer's room, Anna felt afraid of her own sense of desolation, fearing to weep, to make a scene that would upset Marcia.

It surprised her to find the First Lady propped up on a great many snowy pillows, frail, translucent-looking and yet full of a gentle, glowing kind of life.

'You were out of London?' Marcia asked, patting a place on the bed where Anna was to sit. 'They tell me you've broken off from James.'

'Yes. I realised it wouldn't do. I don't love him enough.'

'And you know what the real thing is like.'

'Yes,' Anna said. It was enough; Marcia understood. For a moment the woman lay still against the soft pillows, her dark eyes enormous in the face so much wasted by illness. She was very beautiful, Anna thought; it was as though so little of her flesh remained that there was nothing to obscure the spirit which shone through.

'Give Alexei another chance,' the dancer said at last with a weak urgency. 'You must begin again with him now that you are free. Let him know that you need him. You have to conquer his pride and fear.'

'But he — ' protested Anna, remembering how in Paris he had looked at her, how coldly he had dismissed her. 'He doesn't want me.'

'Go to him. Try. Make him want you.'

'How?' It was what Helen Martineau had said, exactly the same.

'You must! Go down, now; find

Max.' Quite suddenly the frail flame of strength was extinguished; she lay back, white as the pillows themselves, tiny and exhausted. In fear Anna got to her feet and hurried downstairs to find Max; she rushed into the room overlooking the garden, and he was there — in company with the magnificent figure of Alexei Baran.

The room seemed too small. Hardly able to get out the words, Anna said, 'Max, she needs you — she's so weak — '

Max went at once, saying nothing, and Anna found herself alone, unbearably alone with the man she so terribly and hopelessly loved. She trembled, and wished herself anywhere else in the world.

12

For a few moments she could not bring herself to meet his eyes, nor could she find anything at all to say. She stood mute and helpless, feeling the air all about them throbbing with tension. The thought came to her that he might suspect her of having manoeuvred their meeting, and this at last stung her into agitated and incoherent speech.

'How could I have known you'd be here? I didn't mean — '

'I assure you, nor did I.' The formidable coldness of his soft voice did nothing to lessen her discomfort.

'I was out of town. Max wrote, and I came.'

'I also have just come — from Paris.'

Was there a slight emphasis on the word 'Paris'? Did he mean to remind her?

'And how is James?' he then said, and

294

she understood that, of course, he had their last meeting in mind — and realised also that he had most probably drawn conventional but in fact erroneous conclusions about her presence there with James.

'He's well, I suppose,' she said stiffly. 'And he's free, if that's of any interest. How is Kirilova?'

He ignored the question. 'Then there is at least some sense in your head!' He had turned away from her and was looking out over the drab grey and yellow-brown of the garden, where rose bushes stood heavy with recent rain, their last late blooms beaten to the earth. Anna could not see his face and could only guess at the expression on it. He seemed angry, restless, all the time on the verge of sudden violent movement as though the room were a prison to him and her presence an irritant; his very stillness disturbed the air, being so unnatural and so hard to maintain. He was utterly a creature of the theatre, she thought; he had too much presence, too much magnetism about him for every-day existence. The perception filled her with unhappiness, confirming the great and irreconcilable difference between them. His world was other than hers.

'Go to him. Make him want you,' Marcia had said. But what was the use to either of them of wanting? What good would come of his wanting her, even supposing that she had the least power to make him do so? And yet she loved him now as much and as painfully as she had done since that night when they had walked together about the streets of London — and since before that, perhaps ever since she had looked through the lens of her camera at his face in the light of a September morning, and had taken prisoner his image. That had been the very first moment, the moment at which she had reached out from her own restricted world and had taken hold on the substance of all her dreams.

'My life must be very hard for you to imagine,' she said now, wanting to defend herself and yet not knowing how. 'We are so far apart. Nothing's valid for both of us — there's no meeting-place.'

'How can there be? You are all planned, all conventions. I belong to a world of illusion, there is no substance to me.'

He was saying again, as he had done at the airport, that there was no place in his life for love of any woman. The small hope that had struggled for life in Anna's heart died now. Marcia was wrong; there was no way to make him want her.

'So,' he said, 'you will marry James, and your life will be settled. You will go on with your work? You have now some success, I understand.'

'I owe you everything for that.'

'No — you owe Lensky a great deal. Had I had any say in the matter you would never have published those pictures of me.' He spoke very matter-of-factly in his soft, accented way, as though much concerned to be scrupulously accurate and fair, to make absolutely clear that there was not even so small a link between them. 'You owe me nothing,' he insisted. 'I do not like to collect debts.'

'Not even so small an obligation? Well, then, I won't burden you with my gratitude. All the same, I shall feel as I wish.'

'You will make a brilliant career. I wish you well.' Suddenly he turned towards her, looking resolutely, directly into her eyes. The muscles of his face were taut as though he held himself with difficulty in check; the lines from the nostrils to the corners of the wide, sensuous mouth seemed to be more deeply scored than she had ever seen them. The look he gave her was level, long, and she could not at all read its meaning, only fearing that she saw somewhere in the depths of his grey eyes a great contempt, a final dismissal.

She could not bear it any longer.

'Tell Max I'll come again,' she blurted out, and turned abruptly from him and went with quick, awkward steps from the room, out of the house, stumbling and running down the drive until she reached the safety of the road, and not caring that he should have seen that she was in flight.

One had very little pride left, she thought on the train back to central London. There wasn't any place for pride in loving someone, and yet somehow it would intrude, there was always a need to save face when things went wrong. She and Baran were both proud. If they had not been, perhaps it would have been possible for them to talk to one another like reasonable beings, and to understand each other a little better. She knew that there could be gentleness in him, and understanding — she had found them both when they had walked and talked together that night. But then passion had come between them, destroying the balance, and everything had gone wrong. Love was a destructive force; she felt confirmed in all her ancient cynicism.

Back at her flat she wondered quite

how she was to face Nina. The tall
house was very quiet, only the offices
downstairs making their usual shrilling
and clatter. Her flat seemed alien
somehow, empty, its strong dark colours
very strange after the cosy, flowery
clutter of the décor at Mrs Baines'. She
wandered about, unpacking bit by bit,
inspecting the food situation in the
kitchen. She might as well stay, now;
she might as well be wretched here as
anywhere. At least it was her own. One
could not run away from unhappiness;
wherever she went she would carry it
with her. And here at least she had
a career — as Baran had said, a
successful one, or at any rate promising
success. She would stay; she would
carry on with the books she was doing
with James, and everything would be
much as before — except that Nina and
James would be happier. It was quite
simple, really.

Convinced of this, she went downstairs to see if Nina was at home. The
little dancer greeted her with joy, with

reproaches, with a passionate outburst of self-condemnation and guilt, until Anna felt quite guilty herself for being the cause of so much energetic soul-searching.

'Honestly, Nina,' she protested, 'you've done me a great kindness. I would have been miserable married to James! I can see that, now. I've never known the least thing about him, he's a total stranger to me still. Think how ghastly to have married him! But with you it's the real thing; you'll both be happy, and so will I because I love you both.'

'Ah, you are so good, so generous, Anna! And I deserve only your loathing and contempt — for I feel that I cheated you, I was underhand and deceitful — '

'No — really. You must have tried not to let it happen, I'm sure of that. But one simply can't do anything about it once it's taken hold.'

'I was *désolée*,' Nina confessed. 'I didn't know what to do — I liked coming here, and yet I didn't dare come for fear of seeing him, and the more I saw him the more I loved him. Fancy — I, who did not believe in love!'

'So much for Lensky! All the same, what about him? Won't you lose your place in the company if you marry James?'

'I am not sure — but I think James may talk him round. James, you know, is very persuasive in his quiet way. And then the First Lady will speak for us — ah, but have you seen her?'

'Just now. I came on here from Richmond.' Anna wanted not to have to think about that — neither about Max and Marcia nor about Baran. But Nina was insistent.

'Such a little, ordinary cold, but she tried to go on working with it, and being tired and unhappy — bronchitis, pneumonia ... But they say she will recover. Tell me, Anna — was he there? Did you see Baran?'

'I saw him,' said Anna shortly, feeling her throat close up under the pressure of tears.

'And is there really no hope that you and he . . . ?'

'None. None whatsoever.'

Nina sighed, shaking her head in vexation.

'The First Lady thought otherwise. And so did I. Can we both have been mistaken? And even James had begun to believe — '

James, when he came to tea with Nina, was glad to find Anna there, and kissed her hands and thanked her.

'We must have been very stupid to let you discover so soon what we had only just found out for ourselves,' he said. 'I'm deeply sorry that it should have happened that way.'

'I overheard you talking in the kitchen. I'm glad, really; it effectively and very quickly ended a false and dangerous situation. I feel much clearer in the head now.'

'Will you at least keep the ring? It sounds silly, but — Anna, I'm glad to have been engaged to you, even though it didn't work out. It's flattering to my ego that you should have considered me at all possible.'

She was touched and amused by this way of looking at it. They were good friends, she thought; even if she had gained nothing else, she had them and they were very dear to her. During tea she watched them happy together and yet trying not to let too much happiness show so that it should not contrast too sharply with her loneliness. Even Sonya, who eventually joined them, had at last decided in favour of her enamoured doctor. It was a warm, contented occasion, and Anna was glad for them all, yet in her heart longed to escape so that it would not matter if she wept. Her emotions would take no notice at all of her certainty that she had much to be thankful for.

'Are you dancing tonight?' she asked Nina.

'Oh, yes — tonight we have *La Bayadère* — very oriental. Monseigneur consents that Irina Schwarz dances instead of Blaise — it is her hour of triumph! All the other principals hate her. Won't you come? Anna, sometime you must. Come with James — he has tonight the great honour to share a box with *le Maître* Lensky.'

'Would it be diplomatic?' Anna wondered. 'Lensky isn't any too fond of me.'

'Lensky has seen the first drafts of the ballet book, my girl,' James told her. 'We present the Imperial Ballet as something quite close to his vision of it, and he's pleased with us. I think we might safely take some small liberties.'

'I don't know.' She would not promise; she was pulled two ways. Part of her longed to see the Imperial in action again, especially in *Bayadère*, which she had never seen; the thought of watching Baran in his own element, in the setting that made sense of him, was at once a temptation and a torment. She could not be sure that it would not hurt too much. Yet could the constant pain, the sense of loss which at every moment filled her, be made any worse by seeing him? Was it not some small consolation that she could at least see him in that way?

By the time James called to find out if she had decided, she was ready. She had put on the black kaftan that she had worn for their first evening together at the Imperial; it hung looser now, and with her hair drawn away from her face she looked thin, severe, strikingly handsome.

'Nina's still sure you could have him if you cared enough,' James said to her as they walked over to the theatre. 'And Marcia too thinks that. I don't know how to help — I don't understand what went wrong.'

'He made it very clear that there's no room in his life for anything but dancing. He doesn't want a wife, a home, or even love. Any kind of intensity or permanence frightens him. James, he lives in an unfurnished room, an empty, bare room high above London, with half-packed suitcases always ready, and a picture of Marcia on the wall. She's the only woman he's ever let himself love.'

'Because of her spirit, her wonderful artistry — and because she's safe, she's never demanded anything of him except that he should dance.'

'And that's the only kind of love he has room for.'

'Then why is he so dreadfully unhappy?' asked James unanswerably. 'His loneliness was the first thing about him that you saw.'

Anna could think of no adequate reply. Baran was unhappy, of course — but maybe the deprivation he suffered was necessary to a great dancer, to a really great artist in any field. One travelled best alone — and Baran travelled all the time.

Lensky came into the box where they were already settled just as the curtain rose. In the gleam of light cast out from the stage he bent over Anna's hand and kissed it, and his black eyes looked more human than she had ever seen them.

'I salute your genius!' he murmured. 'You may ask of me what you will.'

Her eyes met James' expressive look, and she wanted to laugh despite the pain in her heart. What if she were to say to Lensky, 'I want your principal dancer'? She might ask, he had said — but he had not promised that she would get what she asked for. She turned her attention to the stage and waited to see Baran, holding herself taut against the pain that must come with him.

When he came on to the stage it was just as it always was in a theatre when he appeared; the air became charged with a more intense excitement, those watching became convinced that they were witnessing an act of real creation, not just an interpretation. It was impossible not to watch him. The steps he danced were those many others had danced, and yet they were more; it all meant more, somehow. Anna silently reproached herself for having ever even fleetingly dreamed that she might have anything to give him, or any claim more important than this. Nothing could be more important — or so one believed, when he danced.

She sat through the evening, through the intervals, not wanting to talk to anyone. Fortunately, Lensky was busy, magnificently sailing into regions backstage when the house lights came up. James went back with him to see Nina. Anna dared not go with them for fear of meeting Baran; the risk appalled her. She did not ever want to meet him again. She would be for the rest of her life one of the crowd in so far as he was concerned — she would watch him from a safe distance as she should have been content to do, and love him, as so many others did, without hope of fulfilment. If one truly and unselfishly loved, then that ought to be enough.

It was a bleak theory, and she did not really believe in her power to pursue so lofty a course. Nevertheless, when the performance was over she determined to lose James, and slipped away from him in the crush, following a movement of people towards a side exit which came out near to the stage door. There a crowd was steadily growing, the young and enthusiastic, the curious, the fanatical, the lovelorn, all waiting for a last glimpse of their idol as he left the theatre. Anna remembered the night when she had first gone backstage, waiting in Marcia's dressing-room for the Baran retinue to have made an exit. Before that night she herself had sometimes stood outside in the crowd. She had thought then never to do so again; she had thought herself carried with one swift leap over the gulf between the dancers and their public. She had been looking forward, even though with a certain dread, to her first real meeting with Baran. How long ago it seemed!

She was jostled and elbowed by determined fans, who formed a double rank at the door, leaving space between their lines for people to walk. There were friendly cheers for orchestra and for *corps de ballet* who by now had begun to leave. A restless tension seemed to grow as minutes went by; there were bursts of laughter, snatches of singing, comments on the performance — 'But, my dear, his *grands jetées*, positively into the stratosphere!' . . . ' — really only an excess of animal magnetism — ' . . . 'And then, so they say, he slapped her bottom, dropped her to the boards and stalked off!' . . . 'A curious revival, very much a dancer's vehicle, of course, but then with such dancers — ' . . . 'Did you see those photos of him in the *Sunday News*?' Anna listened, feeling wretchedly apart from it all, feeling that she would never belong either here or inside the great emptying shell of the building where she would so much rather be. She was eternally the child outside, her nose pressed unhappily, longingly to the window . . .

A roar swelled, the crowd began to surge forward. He was there, standing at the top of the steps, looking out over their uplifted faces with sombre eyes, the faintest smile curving his lips in an expression more of disdain, of derision than of pleasure. Magnificently furred, he looked like some Tartar prince from continents and centuries distant, a dangerous lord exacting slavish devotion from his subjects, whose worth he placed scarcely higher than that of the beasts they tended. It was a superb act, Anna thought — it was natural to him so to present himself, continuing in the theatrical image; and the fans delighted in it, knowing as well as he did that it was an act and yet willing to suspend disbelief because it was just what they wanted.

He began to come down the steps, to let clutching fingers seize his hands, waving away programmes hopefully thrust at him, touching a pretty face here, smiling on another there. Anna, watching and holding back from the urgent forward thrust of the crowd, found herself all at once pushed off balance and thrown against someone who violently pushed back so that had it not been for the lack of space to do so she would quite literally have fallen at Baran's feet. Helplessly she grabbed at his coat for support, and her face sank into the rich, soft darkness of the fur.

He stopped moving, and his arm went round her.

'You are not hurt?' There was a perceptible tremor in his voice and in the arm that supported her. She dared to look up now into his face, to meet the fierce fire and ice of those grey eyes.

'Not by the crowd,' she said, and felt the words welling out of her, desperate, unstoppable. 'Not by them — only by you. You hurt me more than anything. I can't bear the pain of not daring to love you.'

It was as though the world faded; the crowd became distant, painted paper figures with no sound coming from their open mouths. His eyes looked down through hers, down into the depths of her mind and heart; they

313

seemed to look with longing, half-fearing what they might yet read there.

'Come with me,' he demanded after an endless moment. 'We must make one another understand.'

Then the noise of the crowd was all around them again, a meaningless jabbering pointed with exclamations and sudden cries and laughter. Somehow he guided her through the press of curious people; somehow they reached the car which waited by the kerb at the front of the theatre. Anna climbed into it, and with a rustle of furs he followed; they were at last alone together as the chauffeured limousine slid out into the street.

She was trembling now and did not know what to say to him, could not make herself look into his eyes. But there was no need; very gently he turned her towards him and tilted back her head, and then touched his lips to hers. He smelt faintly still of grease-paint, and of leather and furs; he felt, as her arms of their own accord went round him, strong and safe, and at the same time very dangerous.

'Oh, I don't care about anything — I want you!' she cried helplessly. 'Even if there's no future in it, no room for me in your life, if you want me only sometimes, only in passing — '

'My life,' he said against her lips, 'my life must change. For this also has its demands and its own validity. I need you.'

'Then why, why did it all go so wrong?'

'Because of what I am. I thought you had chosen James, because he offered you security, and you need security. I thought I could never give you anything like that. But then, at the airport, I asked you to wait — remember? You didn't — you never came to the theatre again, and Lensky told me the date for your marriage was fixed, so — I put you out of my mind. Or tried to. How could I have offered you security, Anna? Or any settled kind of life — you know how I live. And then — ah, seeing you

315

with him in Paris, I thought — '

'Oh, I know what you thought then! But it wasn't true. I never loved James in that way. I thought I wanted security, but I don't — I want blind, total love such as I feel for you! It's all that really matters, even if it hurts me every day of my life.'

'It is a gamble, a terrible tempting of providence. Anna, if we should marry, what then? You with your talent, your career, which must continue — yes, I insist, for without it you would be wasted and unhappy — and then I, with my constant travelling, my hours and hours in the theatre, sometimes living in one country for months, then another — ' He shook his head, looking with a kind of despair into her eyes, and yet at the same time laughing because they both knew that they would marry despite all that. 'What kind of a marriage? How would we escape the miseries of jealousy, the tedium of separation?'

'But think of the reunions! And we'd

never become bored from seeing too much of one another, would we?'

'We don't know one another at all.'

'We've known one another for ever. You can't escape, Alexei, however hard you try. Oh, I shall always be so jealous!'

'And I — always, jealous — ' Suddenly, fiercely he kissed her with an intense and angry passion, as though he would punish her even now for future pain, for his loss of freedom. 'And children?' he demanded at last. 'Are we to have them? And what in the world will they be like?'

'Oh — I don't know, I hadn't thought that far.' She could feel no need for a child, not seeing how such lives as they must lead had any room for children. But one day perhaps she would feel differently. 'We shall have money,' she said tentatively. 'If — when — if we had a child, we would have to buy security for it. Nannies, a house, such things that can be bought. We could give love.'

'So strange to think of. I never before thought about it.'

'It's all strange.' Weakly she leaned against him, feeling the hot tears at last begin to rise — tears of an intense emotion, past unhappiness, present unbelief. 'Alexei, is it true? Will you really marry me? You don't have to.'

'But I do. I have to marry you. I want to marry you. You are to be my anchor to the world, you are that without which I would become so deep in isolation that soon no one would reach me. Besides, quite simply, I want you, I have fallen in love with you like any other man, and it is foolish too long to argue with love.' A smile such as she had never seen lit his eyes. His face in the changing lights from outside the moving car seemed younger, happier than she had ever seen it, and familiar as though she had known it from the beginning of her life.

'It's all because I captured your image,' she said, daring to tease him. 'I stole your soul and made it prisoner in a little box, and now you'll never get free.'

'Keep the image — keep it in your heart, always, and I won't want to be free. I shall know that I am safe. Then nothing else will matter — we can be ourselves, follow our separate careers, and still we shall belong together.' Then there were no more words as he kissed her, and she clung to the great warmth and strength of him, and knew that despite themselves somehow the future would come right. This was what mattered, this blaze of recognition, of certainty, of love. The rest of life would follow, the seasons and the years, and because love would direct them it would all be well.

THE END

We do hope that you have enjoyed reading this large print book.

Did you know that all of our titles are available for purchase?

We publish a wide range of high quality large print books including:
Romances, Mysteries, Classics
General Fiction
Non Fiction and Westerns

Special interest titles available in large print are:
The Little Oxford Dictionary
Music Book, Song Book
Hymn Book, Service Book

Also available from us courtesy of Oxford University Press:
Young Readers' Dictionary
(large print edition)
Young Readers' Thesaurus
(large print edition)

For further information or a free brochure, please contact us at:
Ulverscroft Large Print Books Ltd.,
The Green, Bradgate Road, Anstey,
Leicester, LE7 7FU, England.
Tel: (00 44) **0116 236 4325**
Fax: (00 44) **0116 234 0205**

Other titles in the
Linford Romance Library:

SEASONS OF CHANGE

Margaret McDonagh

When Kathleen Fitzgerald left Ireland twenty years ago, she never planned to return. In England she married firefighter Daniel Jackson and settled down to raise their family. However, when Dan is injured in the line of duty, events have a ripple effect, bringing challenges and new directions to the lives of Dan, Kathleen and their children, as well as Kathleen's parents and her brother, Stephen. How will the members of this extended family cope with their season of change?

CHERRY BLOSSOM LOVE

Maysie Greig

Beth was in love with her boss, but he could only dream of the brief passionate interlude he had shared with a Japanese girl long ago, and of the child he had never seen. Beth agrees to accompany him to Japan in search of his daughter. There perhaps, the ghost of Madame Butterfly would be laid, and he would turn to her for solace . . . Her loyal heart is lead along dark and dangerous paths before finding the love she craves.

0	1	2	3	4	5	6	7	8	9
7670	901		3173	70x		346	501	1588	339
	861			9744	9725		127	968	9529
	0771						9587		
							3087		
								7978	

P10-L2061